Alien Abattoir
and Other Stories

by Sean Patrick Hazlett

Dedication

To my wife Claire, for putting up with my flights of fancy and reading my stories when they were more flawed and far less polished.

Table of Contents

Acknowledgements

I would like to thank all the teachers and writers that helped me along the way, or, barring that, did not discourage me when they by all rights should have. My fifth grade teacher, Mrs. Umile, was instrumental in encouraging me to write my first fantasy stories regaling her with the adventures of Draclot and Lord Spaz. I want to thank internationally best-selling novelist David Vann for having patience with some of my early writing while I was a Stanford undergraduate. David had encouraged his students to take his creative writing course with the pass/no credit option so they'd feel more comfortable experimenting with different literary styles. I want to thank him for his advice, especially since my early work was terrible and I had no business being in the same room with someone as talented as David. Yet he never discouraged me and always provided productive critiques that helped me improve my work. Best-selling author Jeff Carlson inspired me to write fiction after sharing his wisdom and experience. He also graciously took the time to critique one of my stories, pointing out all the rookie mistakes I'd been making early in my writing career. Lastly, I want to thank award-winning author and editor, Nick Mamatas, for his unvarnished and relentless critiques of several of my stories. Most people hold back their criticism, but Nick never candy-coated his feedback. Because of it, he made me a better writer. He also taught plenty of techniques that really helped me hone my craft. In the end, I doubt I will ever reach Nick's bar for excellence, but he definitely set a high standard to which I can aspire.

Introduction

This anthology includes ten short stories I wrote from the end of 2011 through early 2013. Many of them have already appeared in venues such as *Fictionvale Magazine*, *Mad Scientist Journal*, *NewMyths.com*, *Plasma Frequency Magazine*, *Outposts of Beyond*, and *The Colored Lens*, while others have garnered Honorable Mentions in the Writers of the Future Contest. They cover concepts as varied as biological computing, space colonization gone horribly awry, ancient alien astronauts, interstellar investment banking, and alternative history, among others.

While I've been writing since I was ten years old, I only began a serious effort to publish my stories in the last few months of 2011. The one great thing about short stories is that they are useful media for generating and validating ideas. They allow writers to test concepts relatively quickly without the time and commitment required to write a novel. Additionally, they also provide writers with an opportunity to learn and experiment with the craft of fiction writing.

Over the last few years, I've learned a lot and have had a great deal of fun bringing these new worlds to life. I plan on creating many more in the future. I hope you enjoy reading these tales as much as I've loved writing them.

Enemy Allies

Georg Strauss was lost. The dense iron ore deposits embedded in the region's crust rendered his compass useless. *"Magnetic interference,"* the High Command had said. The stalks of corn, vast rolling hills and ridges, and thick smoke and fog made map navigation challenging. Everything looked the same.

Aside from thousands of bloated bodies littering the battlefield, the only things distinguishing this specific spot were the peculiar Soviet soldiers he'd observed dragging German corpses up a nearby hill. A dull yellow light pulsed like a homing beacon from beyond the hill's crest.

The soldiers moved with a stiff walk, like automatons with an unnaturally cadenced gait. Strauss had seen many strange things during his time on the Eastern Front, but never something quite so unnerving.

A waxing moon held vigil over the dark dull gray sky. *Is it any wonder that the Russian soul was so bleak, ever embracing oblivion?* Strauss slogged onward.

The air reeked of cordite, burning diesel, and charred flesh. Exposure to this toxic stew gave him a headache, while the scent of roasting meat only made him hungrier. Strauss's mouth was dry. Cottonmouth was a side effect of the Pervitin tablets, which had kept him awake for the past three days. But, he needed to sleep soon. Otherwise, the hallucinations would start again. Even with methamphetamines, the human body couldn't persist for long without sleep.

Strauss rubbed the scars on his left arm. He'd suffered third-degree burns in '42—wounds that had saved his life.

Those had been dark days. Fighting block by block in the streets and crawling through the sewers, killing Russians with his brother, Heinz. It was an experience he would never forget. Dirty work, that. Ivan would sometimes get close. So close Strauss could smell the borscht and vodka on his breath. Strauss had had to use the bayonet more than once. When you open a man's gut and his intestines spill out, it doesn't smell pretty. The "War of the Rats," the newspapers had called it, because rats were what the soldiers in the sewers had become. Strauss's injury had placed him on the last medical flight out of Stalingrad before the weather turned sour and the Soviets had encircled the Sixth Army.

Heinz hadn't made it. Neither did anyone else from Strauss's tiny Bavarian town. Strauss was the lone survivor. The Wehrmacht didn't have an individual replacement system like the well-supplied Yanks. That's why German soldiers formed stronger bonds with one another. It's why they fought better and harder than any other military on earth. At least that's how the High Command justified a recruitment policy that left entire towns devoid of German manhood.

As Strauss trudged across the loamy earth, he followed the deep tread marks that forged a path through a cornfield. The path widened into low-lying grassland that rose up a gently sloping knoll. To his west rested a disabled fifty-six-ton Tiger tank. Its treads were shredded, but the armor on its hull and turret had suffered no signs of penetration.

Strauss climbed on the Tiger to check for survivors. When he reached the tank's turret, he saw that one of its two hatches was open. He peered inside, but the crew appeared to have abandoned the tank some time ago.

There was nothing for him here. The answers he sought lay beyond the knoll. Strauss dismounted the tank, and began his slow ascent up the hill.

The wind swirled around him, carrying the stench of death and burning petrol. The cornfields had protected him from the worst of it. Now he was in the open. Soon the moisture on the ground would accelerate the decomposition of the corpses surrounding him. Strauss yawned and rubbed his eyes. He needed to take sleep before sleep took him.

Despair had been a constant companion for so many years he could barely remember a life without it. Sometimes he asked himself if such a life was worth suffering for. He envied Heinz. An infamous Soviet sniper – a woman, no less – had blown his brains out in Stalingrad. At least Heinz's torment was over. For Strauss, it never ended.

As Strauss neared the pinnacle, he lowered himself and crawled forward. The stench of death grew fouler, ripe with decay and putrefaction.

His heart raced as he peeked over the other side, expecting to find the Soviets in a reverse slope defense. Instead, he spied an impact crater about four hundred meters across, with a maximum depth of roughly thirty meters. At its center, a cylindrical structure protruded from a midnight-black disk. An earthen ramp extended from the disk's edge to the south-facing wall.

In the crater, scores of German and Soviet soldiers carried dark gray minerals from a mine shaft near the east-facing wall to the black structure. Even more disconcerting to Strauss was that aside from their footfalls, the soldiers made no sound.

As Strauss looked more closely at the men, his apprehension deepened. Some had missing limbs; others, exposed bone. All had the gray-green skin of corpses. Strauss's instinctive terror wrestled with disbelief. *No, this can't be real. I must be hallucinating.*

One of the dead things swiveled its head toward Strauss, its glowing yellow eyes betraying it as something other than human. A rush of panic threatened to overwhelm him. Strauss shivered. With one fluid motion, the walking corpse swung its rifle to its hip and fired.

Strauss hit the ground. A sharp, white-hot pain seared through his left shoulder. He grabbed his shoulder in a futile effort to compress the smoldering wound. Strauss gritted his teeth and grunted. The bullet burned. Below, more Soviet and German soldiers had turned and were approaching his position. All had glowing yellow eyes. The surreal sight shook Strauss to the core.

જી

Eight days earlier - 0630 Hours, 4 July 1943, near Belgorod, Russia

One hundred soldiers and officers bearing the skull and crossbones insignia of the Third SS Totenkopf Panzergrenadier Division formed a horseshoe around SS-Hauptsturmführer Krüger, commander of Ninth Company, Third SS Panzer Regiment.

Krüger stood before a detailed topographic map of the Kursk salient papered on the wall of a dilapidated Russian farmhouse. The salient marked the west-facing bulge of the German-Soviet front lines around the city of Kursk. Threshers, reapers, and a four-row tractor lay idle in the cornfield beyond. To the right of the salient, dozens of red icons dotted the map, each one representing a Soviet Army equivalent. On the left, blue icons designated dozens of German divisions.

"Tomorrow at oh-three-thirty hours, Ninth Company will form in column in its designated assembly area. Simultaneously, Fourth Panzer Army aviation assets and division artillery will pound Soviet strong points, softening 'em up for our assault, which will commence at oh-four-hundred hours.

"Our division has the covering mission for the Second SS Panzer Corps' northern flank. As our company is the division's only heavy Tiger I unit, we will spearhead the attack in an armored wedge. Scouts report multiple, concentric defensive belts ringed with mines, heavy artillery, T-34 tanks, and antitank guns. Our superior armor and firepower will draw enemy fire while our sister companies breach Soviet defenses.

"The Wehrmacht's objective for Operation Citadel is to cut off upwards of two million Soviet troops, five thousand enemy tanks, and twenty-five thousand guns and mortars in the Kursk bulge. As part of the Fourth Panzer Army, we will proceed north, establishing a bridgehead across the Psel River, and advancing toward Prokhorovka.

"Take initiative and be aggressive. Don't fall for Ivan's treachery. If he surrenders, be vigilant. Check for grenades. Watch your backs. I will see you on the high ground." Krüger dropped his arms to his side, and kicked his feet together in a rigid position. "Company! Ach...tung!"

The entire company snapped to attention.

"My honor is loyalty!" Krüger yelled.

"My honor is loyalty!" the men echoed.

"Dis...Missed."

Men scrambled to their tanks, grease guns in-hand. They inspected their tracks, knowing from experience that an immobile tank was a fighting coffin. They oiled their machine guns and boresighted their main cannons. They replaced broken gearboxes, fixed damaged idler arms, and fueled their tanks with diesel. The battalion surgeon distributed Pervitin tablets in anticipation of a week's worth of continuous combat without sleep.

Strauss felt out of place among the Waffen SS. Most had volunteered for this insanity. He was surrounded by stiff and fanatical Prussians who strutted about as if they actually believed the master race garbage Hitler fed them. Strauss made it into the elite unit's ranks not because he was particularly loyal or zealous, but because he had an unusual talent for killing Ivan. His actions in the Stalingrad sewers were legendary, even more so since he was a trained Panzergrendier, not an infantryman.

Only two things caught the Waffen SS's eye – impeccable loyalty or battlefield competence. Soldiers rarely possessed both. Strauss exemplified the latter.

Officers were the exception, displaying both tactical proficiency and fanaticism. Every SS officer had to pass an intense combat course where he engaged in death-defying feats like digging foxholes in front of advancing tanks. Those who failed died.

Soldiers with time and paper often spent their final minutes before sleep writing letters home. For Strauss, it was all a farce. The SS censored most correspondence, so what was the point? No one could possibly understand this hyper-Darwinian hell, so why bother attempting to describe it? Few soldiers would return home alive, anyway.

As dusk approached, dark gray, swollen rain clouds gathered on the horizon, threatening to burst. As twilight dovetailed into night, a sliver of lightning tore across the sky, illuminating the bleak landscape's hopeless infinity. The heavens opened up, inundating the expectant combatants as thunder roared in the distance.

Soon another kind of thunder erupted. Hundreds of Stuka dive-bombers, sirens whining, unloaded their deadly ordnance on the Soviets. Dozens of explosions rippled across the skyline. Minutes later, the division ground batteries opened up, blasting Soviet positions with tons of heavy artillery.

ဆ

Thirteen hours ago - 0830 Hours, 12 July 1943, outside Prokhorovka, Russia

Strauss's company had survived over one week of hellish combat, fighting through two concentric Soviet defensive belts. Now it prepared to penetrate a third ring on the outskirts of Prokhorovka.

The advance coincided with the Luftwaffe's bombing of Soviet positions. As Strauss's unit maneuvered in a tight wedge formation, the Soviets responded to the aerial bombardment with a surprise of their own, launching the blistering fire of Katyusha rockets and heavy artillery.

Strauss wiped the sweat dripping into his eyes as he surveyed the battlefield through the gunner's primary sight. He felt claustrophobic in the cramped gunner's station.

"Unteroffizier Meier," Strauss said to his tank commander. "We should stop and scan for enemy tanks. This ground favors the defender. Ivan's probably got something waiting for us ahead. We could be stumbling into an ambush."

Meier scoffed. "You heard our orders, Strauss. We are to stop for nothing, even if Ivan immobilizes one of our other tanks. We must maintain our momentum."

"Yes, Unteroffizier." Strauss knew from experience not to challenge Meier. The SS had obviously selected him for loyalty, not sill.

The tense moments before an engagement pumped Strauss full of adrenaline, and helped distract him from his extreme exhaustion. He had only eight Pervitin tablets left. He had to make them count.

"Driver! Stop! Now!" Meier exclaimed. "Ivan's counterattacking. T-34s are advancing toward our position."

The tank ground to a halt, and Strauss scanned for targets. "They're moving too fast for me to get a good read on them. They're trying to close in to reduce our range and armor advantages. That's what I'd do. Ivan learns fast."

Meier was not amused. "I don't want to hear excuses or adoration for these subhumans. Focus on knocking out their tanks."

"Two Tanks! Eight hundred meters! Right tank!" Meier barked.

The crew spun into action.

"Identified!" Strauss announced as he centered the T-34 in his sights.

The loader shoved a round into the main gun's breech, "Up!"

"Fire!" Meier ordered once the loader was out of the main gun's path of recoil.

"On the way!" Strauss pulled the trigger and the armor-piercing round sped toward the T-34, exploding its turret on impact.

"Target! Left tank!" Meier commanded.

"Scanning!" Strauss wheeled the main gun left, and then adjusted its elevation. "Identified!"

"Up!"

"Fire!"

"On the way!"

"Target! Cease fire. Gunner, continue to scan."

Burning T-34 hulks littered the battlefield. Smoke blanketed the low ground, making it difficult for gunners to identify more targets.

High-pitched whistles heralded the launch of Soviet artillery. The key to survival was now a rapid advance through the valley.

On his right flank, Strauss spotted a camouflaged Soviet antitank gun. Breaking chain of command protocol, he yelled, "Driver! Turn right!" Any second of delay could prove fatal. The Tiger needed to position its front glacis, where the armor was thickest, toward the enemy's gun. As the tank reoriented itself, an enemy round slammed against its hull. The impact's vibration deafened the crew and shook loose flakes of interior paint onto the men, but the round barely scratched the Tiger's armor.

The tank destroyed the gun and its crew. It then continued advancing, knocking out several more enemy targets. Nevertheless, the Red Army horde seemed to have inexhaustible armor reserves. The frequency of rounds hitting the Tiger accelerated. It was only a matter of time before the Soviets surrounded the Tigers.

"Misfire!" Strauss warned when his last round in the breech malfunctioned.

"Abandon tank!" Meier ordered.

Strauss moved by reflex, without thinking. As he evacuated the vehicle, he saw the Tiger's main gun riddled with coin-sized holes. It was only a matter of time before the unexploded round detonated, blowing them all to oblivion.

As the five men tried to scramble out of the Tiger, Soviet machine gunners cut down three men including Meier, the loader, and the radio operator. The driver never made it out of his hole as a Russian sniper separated the man's head from his body.

Strauss rushed toward the nearest ditch. Upon arrival, he regretted his decision. Blood-drenched bodies littered the field, and the air was thick with flies and other carrion feeders. The stench of death was overwhelming. Thick smoke from burning metal hulks engulfed the battlefield. The only Germans surrounding him were dead.

The ground vibrated as Soviet armor lumbered across the plain. The Red Army had launched a counteroffensive with tens of thousands of men, armor, and materiel pouring through the area.

Strauss had three options: surrender, fight until dead, or hide. Only one offered him a chance at survival. Crawling into the bloody morass of German corpses, Strauss played dead.

He lay there for hours, choking back vomit as the bodies ripened under a sweltering summer sun. Biting horse flies had their way with him. Rats nipped at his limbs and torso. This was the sort of death he had most feared, slow and painful.

Toward the evening, echelon after echelon of Soviet regiments passed him by, underscoring a crushing defeat for the Wehrmacht. The advancing Soviets paid no heed to the German dead. They'd likely relegate the burial duties to local civilians, or so Strauss hoped. At nightfall, he would make his way back to German lines.

By dusk, smoke still blanketed the battlefield, but most of the Soviet formations had advanced farther west. All was quiet, but the stillness was nothing but the eye of a storm. Strauss heard scraping sounds ahead. They were barely audible at first, but grew louder as their source drew closer.

Strauss pushed a corpse aside, and lifted his head out of the mire to determine the cause of the commotion.

He noticed a silhouette of a Russian soldier standing one hundred meters away, juxtaposed against the smoky haze. The soldier was dragging a German corpse out of the ditch and toward a nondescript knoll. Other Soviet soldiers performed the same gruesome task.

Strauss found the soldiers' silence disturbing. Not a whisper passed among them, yet they worked like well-coordinated drones.

Why don't they just bury the bodies in place?

Strauss feared the Soviets would soon discover him during their macabre undertaking, but curiosity got the better of him. He decided to investigate.

He crept through the gully, hiding beneath bodies whenever the Soviets returned. In the darkness, he never saw their faces, only a preternatural yellow glow.

The ditch opened up into a vast cornfield obscuring his vision, yet he could still see the knoll in the distance. As he stole through the field, he discovered the tracks of a Tiger tank, which he followed. Without stalks of corn to obstruct his path, he'd be less likely to stumble into an ambush.

ᛒ

Present time - 2130 Hours, 12 July 1943, near Prokhorovka, Russia

Despite the pain from the bullet wound in his shoulder, Strauss's training took over. He rolled away from the crater's edge and sprinted toward the Tiger. He climbed on the tank's turret, opened a hatch, and lowered himself into the commander's cupola. Protected by the tank's thick armor, Strauss closed the hatch and loaded the tank's 7.92-millimeter coaxial machine gun.

Scores of German and Soviet soldiers climbed out of the crater. They advanced on his position with calm efficiency. Bullets passed into the tank's tiny gun port, glancing off Strauss's helmet. Strauss's hands shook as he wiped a bead of sweat dripping from his brow. His attackers' uncanny accuracy terrified him. *Keep it together, man. Keep it together.*

Strauss unloaded his machine gun in three-round bursts. But the corpses kept coming. He struggled to contain an avalanche of doubt and terror. He aimed at their heads. But even when he shattered their skulls, they shambled forward, headless. Strauss wavered. He wanted to flee, but if he did, they'd almost certainly kill him out in the open.

Strauss closed his eyes and took a deep breath. *Think, man. Think.* He stared through the tank's sights, watching the dead surge inexorably forward. Frantic, he took another deep breath.

He aimed for their legs, hoping to immobilize them. The tactic slowed their progress, but still they crawled forward. Strauss exhaled. *Progress.* It took half an hour to disable about forty of them, his machine gun ripping their wriggling limbs to shreds.

He waited desperately, fearing another attack from the crater. None came. Terror kept him vigilant, temporarily pushing away the siren song of sleep. He foraged through the turret for rounds, food, or anything else that might help him survive, and found a map with the knoll circled in red.

After full darkness descended, he left the turret's protection, and dropped down to the radio operator's compartment on the hull to call for help. Strauss knew he'd be transmitting a message in the clear. Without encryption, the Soviets would likely intercept it. Strauss didn't care. Better the Soviets than some unknown and unnatural threat.

Strauss switched on the wireless. "Any station, any station, this is Georg Strauss, Ninth Company, Third SS Panzer Regiment. Request immediate assistance. Over."

Silence.

He tried again.

A voice with a heavy Russian accent responded in German. "Fascist invader, this is Soviet transmitting station one-zero-three. Relay your coordinates for immediate surrender. Over."

Strauss was starting to regret his decision. *Why should I risk my neck to alert the Soviets? I should just sneak back behind friendly lines and leave this problem to the enemy.*

Strauss considered his options.

"Soviet transmitting station, this is Strauss. Unidentified hostiles of neither Wehrmacht nor Soviet designation near current location. Proceed with caution. Grid follows. Prepare to copy. Over."

"Send it."

Strauss relayed his coordinates to the Soviets, and then returned to the tank's cupola, reloaded the machine gun, and waited for his sworn enemy to arrive.

After a tense hour, a diesel engine rumbled in the distance. The squat silhouette of a T-34 emerged from the south, out of the cornfield. It seemed the trigger-happy Soviets had deliberately avoided the Tiger's trail. Strauss couldn't blame them. He'd set up some nasty ambushes along similar routes.

Strauss counted twelve soldiers crammed on the tank's rear deck. As they got closer, he noticed one was female. He wasn't surprised. The Soviets had employed women to deadly effect at Stalingrad. He knew from personal experience.

The T-34 squealed to a halt about thirty feet from Strauss's Tiger, the engine still running. The tank commander shouted something in Russian. The squad dismounted. Rifles raised, the troops approached Strauss. The T-34's turret swiveled toward the Tiger. Strauss waved a makeshift grayish-white flag fashioned from his filthy undershirt.

One particular brute took no chances. *"Hände hoch!"* he screamed in crude German. Strauss raised his hands above his head in as exaggerated a gesture as possible. Sometimes the Soviets shot first and asked questions later.

Rifle still raised, the man's pace accelerated as he closed in on Strauss's position. When he reached the treads of Strauss's Tiger, he motioned for his squad members to surround the tank. The man slung his rifle over his shoulder and climbed aboard the Tiger.

His face contorted in a sneering rictus, the man slammed the butt of his rifle into Strauss's mouth, knocking loose several teeth. Strauss's eyes watered, his teeth throbbing. *Maybe calling the Soviets wasn't such a great idea.* He spit out blood and cupped his mouth with his hand.

"Nyet!" the woman said. The soldier backed off, but motioned for Strauss to dismount the tank. Dazed from the blow, Strauss had enough sense to comply with the Russian's orders.

In heavily accented German, the woman snarled, "Fascist invader, you are now officially a prisoner of the Red Army. I'm Major Anna Ilyinichna Ivanova, commander of this special detachment. You will answer all questions without hesitation."

Strauss nodded.

"Who are you, and what is your unit designation?"

"Georg Strauss, Ninth Company, Third SS Panzer Regiment."

"Liar!" She slapped Strauss. His head snapped back. The blow stung. *So this is how it's gonna be.*

"Please. There's no time for this. There are reanimated dead in a crater beyond that knoll." Strauss pointed toward the crater.

Strauss's attempt to take control of the interrogation triggered another slap. "You see this man here, the one who knocked out your teeth?" She gestured toward the brute. "Fascists raided his village outside of Smolensk in

'41. After they killed his parents and razed his home, they raped his sister. He wants to gut you like a chicken. I urge you to cooperate."

"Please, just hear me out," Strauss said.

"Fine. Tell me the truth about your actual unit and I'll listen."

"I'm not lying about my unit."

"Third SS Panzer retreated this afternoon with over seventy-five percent casualties, so you're either a liar or a deserter, and I've never captured a German deserter."

"If you have to put me in the 'deserter' category, so be it."

"Prove you were in that unit."

"Well, my uniform probably won't convince you, because I could've pulled it off a corpse. My outdated company-specific maps likely won't convince you either. It doesn't really matter anyway, since we'll all be dead soon."

That got her attention. "Suppose I believe you. What's on that knoll that has you so scared you're willing to try your luck with the Red Army?"

Strauss told the major his story. Ivanova reacted with a smirk.

"Don't believe me?" he said. "See for yourselves. Be careful, though. The things up there have better aim and reflexes than any sniper I've ever seen—Soviet or German. I suggest you drop every piece of ordnance you have on that crater, 'cause what's inside isn't going to go down easily."

She smiled and said something to her men in Russian. They erupted in laughter. "I told them about your walking dead and your plan to waste the Motherland's artillery on a harmless hill."

Ivanova shouted orders in Russian to a rail-thin soldier. The man rushed forward with a knife and a bottle of vodka. She pointed at the soldier. "Not that he can speak German, nor you Russian, but this is Private Dmitry Severinov."

Fearing the worst, Strauss backed away from the knife-wielding soldier.

She waved her hand. "He's here to remove the bullet from your shoulder. If I wanted you dead, you'd be dead."

The skinny man poured vodka on Strauss's wound. The resulting sting made him wince. Then Severinov used his knife to extract the bullet. The cold knife stung as Severinov drove it deeper into Strauss's shoulder and fished for the burning bullet. Strauss howled. A wave of agony and nausea washed over him.

Ignoring the pain, Strauss tried to address a more pressing matter. "So, you'll do it? You'll call in your artillery?"

Ivanova laughed. "We, Russians, are not so melodramatic. We're not going to shell a hilltop based on some fascist's tall tale, but we did notice both Soviet and German remains scattered around your tank." She pointed at the smoke rising from the corpses. "The bullets are still hot. It's clear you killed other Germans. But why?"

"I already told you."

Ivanova turned and issued more commands. The men grinned. Then six of them slung their rifles over their shoulders and marched toward the hilltop.

They disappeared into the smoky haze while Severinov finished stitching Strauss's wound and bandaged his shoulder. Strauss's wound no longer burned, but it still throbbed.

Ivanova regarded Strauss as if he were a wounded bear. He fixed his attention on the smoky mist, awaiting the inevitable. "We really should be focused on the hill. If your men stir up whatever's in the crater, it's likely to come down here. We should be ready."

Ivanova huffed and shook her head. "If anything happens to my men, I'll shoot you."

A rifle shot rang out in the distance, followed by sporadic small-arms fire. Blood-curdling screams preceded an ominous silence.

"Call for fire support," Strauss said.

"Again, I'm not going to drop artillery based upon enemy recommendations. All seven of us will investigate what happened. Then I'll decide what to do once I have better intelligence."

"Would you at least ask your headquarters to launch an artillery strike in two hours? You can always cancel it before then."

She considered Strauss's proposal. "I'll put a three-hour delay on the strike." Ivanova walked over to the T-34 and accessed its wireless set. She radioed her headquarters and provided the eight-digit grid coordinates. She returned to the six men and said, "Take us to the crater, fascist."

The seven soldiers stumbled through the smoky miasma. Ivanova had pushed Strauss to the front of the column, but refused to provide him with a weapon for self-defense.

The smell of sulfur flooded Strauss's senses. Besides Pervitin and terror, it helped keep him awake. The last thing he wanted was to collapse from exhaustion minutes after confronting some unknown menace, so he downed half of his eight remaining Pervitin tablets.

The acrid smoke burned Strauss's eyes as he ventured deeper into the haze. As they ascended the hill in near blindness, the sound of metal clanging on rock echoed from the crater.

A light breeze pushed a bank of smoke past Strauss. He moved carefully to avoid stumbling into whatever was in the mist beyond. He stepped onto something soft, almost tripping over a body. He raised his right hand to signal a halt. Despite their conflicting allegiance, the six Russians complied. He bent down on one knee to examine the corpse.

The body was still hot. Its right shoulder was bloodied. "A wound like that shouldn't kill a man," Strauss said. Then he noticed the man's head. Its skullcap was cleaved off, and its brain was missing. Horrified, Strauss stumbled backward. What the hell is going on?

"Private Bakunin!" Ivanova gasped. She shuddered as she moved forward to view the body. "What did this?"

Strauss ignored her question. "Drop some rounds in the crater and be done with it."

Ivanova shook her head. "I must see this through. If I bomb this hill without confirming my soldiers' deaths, the commissar will execute me. We must go on."

Strauss sighed.

The group resumed its trek through the smog. Along the way, they discovered more members of the squad, all of whom had nonfatal gunshot wounds. Their skullcaps and brains were missing. Ivanova tabulated her butcher's bill, collecting each soldier's dog tags to protect herself from execution.

As the seven soldiers neared the hilltop, Ivanova grabbed Strauss's arm. "Stop. This isn't everyone."

Shots rang out. Ivanova fell, screaming. Others fell with nary a whimper. A sharp pain ripped through Strauss's shin. A Soviet soldier emerged from the haze, his eyes glowing dull yellow. The soldier lacked a skullcap. More shadows pierced the mist's veil, drawing ever closer. Strauss panicked, struggling to breathe, his vision fading to black.

క్ర

Strauss awoke to a blinding light from above. He lay on a cold metal table. His muscles felt weak and lethargic, as if he'd been drugged with something far stronger than morphine that was only now beginning to wear off. He had a splitting headache coupled with dizziness and nausea.

As Strauss's eyes adjusted to the light, he found himself in a cylindrical room. The chamber's walls seemed filled with a yellow-green fluid. Suspended in that fluid were columns of wrinkled gray ellipsoids. Each object had hundreds of folds, and each throbbed in an eerie cadence in synchronicity with the others.

Mein Gott. Human brains!

A man screamed.

The screeching reverberated throughout the chamber, but originated from a table directly across from him. Strauss looked down the length of his body, past his feet, at the chamber's center. Eight tables radiated from an empty three-meter-diameter circular platform at the chamber's center. The tables were spaced at equal intervals like spokes on a wheel. Ivanova lay unconscious two tables over at Strauss's nine o'clock position.

The remaining five tables were empty. Strauss wondered where the other soldiers were. There was a two-meter-wide gap between their heads and the chamber wall. Behind Severinov's head stood the devil incarnate.

A coal-black squid-like being worked behind Severinov with four of its eight tentacles whirling in motion. Each tentacle ended in four opposable fingers. Eight red eyes conveying a deep and menacing intelligence gazed out from its Volkswagen-sized head. A crimson hourglass-shaped mark dominated the crest of its head. Oily black fluid oozed from its pores. The creature possessed a wide vertical maw lined with rifle-length fangs.

This can't be happening. I must be hallucinating. I have to be. I haven't slept in days.

Beneath Severinov's screams, a faint hissing accompanied a solid shaft of glowing red light boring into Severinov's skull. The screaming abated and a sucking sound followed as one of the creature's tentacles extracted Severinov's gray matter from his open cranium.

The scent of searing human flesh permeated the room and put to rest any doubts Strauss had about what was happening. This nightmare was real. Strauss didn't fear death. But the thought of getting a lobotomy from this squid-thing terrified him.

Throughout the years, Strauss had survived more brushes with death than he could count. He'd hunted and been hunted by people, the most dangerous predators on earth. He was a hardened veteran forged and tempered. But he had never felt as helpless at any point in his life as he did now in this human abattoir.

Then he remembered Heinz and all the other men from his town who'd served with him and died. He owed it to them to survive.

Strauss racked his brain for a suitable course of action. He realized the squid-thing hadn't bothered removing anyone's clothing or equipment with the exception of the soldiers' rifles and pistols. Severinov still had three grenades on a bandolier strapped across his chest. Perhaps the creature only recognized the weapons people had tried to use against it in the past.

The squid-thing turned its back to Strauss and faced the wall. It lifted Severinov's brain high above its head, then deposited it into a small compartment built into the glassy surface.

This is my chance, Strauss thought, only to realize the chamber had no visible exits. The grinding sound of operating hydraulics resonated from the floor. A circular platform rose slowly from the craft's center. When it reached the ceiling, the hydraulic noise stopped for a fleeting moment, and then began anew. As the platform descended, a pair of Wehrmacht-issued steel-toed boots came into view.

The thing shifted its black mass and blood-red eyes toward the platform and lumbered forward, propelled by its hind tentacles. The platform reached the floor. A dead German soldier stood facing Strauss in silence, rifle in hand, and yellow eyes aglow.

Strauss feigned unconsciousness, summoning all the lessons he had learned from his tour in Stalingrad to avoid attracting unwanted attention.

Keeping his eyes barely open, Strauss saw the creature remove the dead German's helmet. Beneath, the man's skullcap appeared fused back to his lower cranium, judging from the thin scar across his forehead. The creature pressed something on the back of the soldier's head, and his skullcap popped open as if on a hinge. It dipped a tentacle into the man's skull and extracted a swarming mass of lice-like organisms. Another tentacle pressed a floor panel. The platform rose again, carrying the soldier with it. After the platform reached the ceiling, it descended, now empty.

The creature turned and shuffled back to Severinov. Amid all the horror, Strauss had forgotten about the artillery. He surreptitiously checked his watch. *Oh, no. Fifteen more minutes.*

The thing inserted the bugs into Severinov's empty cranium and reattached his skullcap. The creature then moved toward the unconscious Ivanova.

The Pervitin must have been potent enough to revive me before the others.

Strauss had to act now.

He swung off the table. His injured right shin ached. The bleeding had stopped, but the wound hurt like hell. He limped toward Severinov. The creature surged forward, grasping at Strauss with its tentacles. Strauss leapt at Severinov's table and grabbed two grenades, one with each hand.

A tentacle twisted around Strauss's leg, hoisting him upside down. Disoriented and nauseated, Strauss nearly emptied his stomach. The creature pulled him toward its face. Its menacing, fierce red eyes gleamed. Strauss struggled to regain his balance. The squid-thing's maw gaped in a shriek. It was the opening Strauss needed.

He raised his right hand to his mouth, pulled the pin with his teeth, and tossed the live grenade into the creature's jaws. The beast gurgled and flailed its tentacles. The whipping tentacle shook him. Strauss hunched over it, trying to find his center. Helpless, he swayed topsy-turvy. His gut roiled. Dizzy, he closed his eyes to avoid vomiting. Then he curled into a ball and braced for an explosion.

The blast hurled Strauss across the chamber. Time slowed as he sailed through the air. He crashed against the glassy wall. The air burst from his lungs. He labored to suck in oxygen, wheezing and on the verge of panic. His ears rang from the explosion, assigning false distance to close sounds. The air reeked of sulfur and burning meat. Black and sticky fluid from the creature's guts soaked him. He wiped his eyes and the blurry film obstructing his vision cleared. Shrapnel holes pitted the walls.

Strauss regained his senses and got back on his feet, thankful the creature's body had absorbed most of the explosive force. The detonation left the tables and the people on them unscathed. Strauss hobbled toward the central platform, frantic to escape before the planned artillery strike. He peered over his shoulder at Ivanova, still lying unconscious on the table.

I can't leave her to die here.

He staggered past Severinov's limp corpse and toward Ivanova.

"Wake up." Strauss tapped his hand on her face. No response. He rifled through his pockets and found the four remaining Pervitin tablets. He grabbed one and shoved it down her throat.

"Wake up!"

He waited for over a minute, his heart pumping as the seconds ticked away. *C'mon. Wake up!*

"Eh?" Ivanova mumbled as she regained consciousness.

"We've got to leave now!" Strauss looked at his watch. "We have three minutes before all hell breaks loose."

She groaned and nodded.

Cold and clammy hands throttled Strauss's neck. Strauss gasped for air. In all the confusion, Severinov must've approached Strauss from behind.

Ivanova yelled in Russian at Severinov, pleading with him.

Strauss dropped his last grenade in an effort to tear Severinov's hands away from his throat. It was no use.

Desperate, Strauss rolled forward, taking Severinov with him. Severinov's body hit the next table with a loud thud. The impact broke Severinov's death grip.

"Ivanova, get the grenade!"

She surged to her feet and ripped the last grenade off Severinov's bandolier, narrowly escaping his thrashing arms. She sprinted to a table opposite hers, pushed it in front of her, and pulled the pin.

"Strauss! Behind the table! Now!"

He hopped past Severinov's reanimated corpse, snatched the other grenade off the floor, and dived behind the table beside Ivanova. She threw her grenade at Severinov. Strauss covered Ivanova with his body. He pulled the table over them both at an angle. The grenade exploded. A concussive bubble blew the table backward, then slammed them against the wall. Smoky shrapnel sprayed the table. Yet the table held firm, protecting Strauss and Ivanova from the white-hot shards of burning metal. Chunks of human flesh splattered the chamber walls.

When the dust settled, Strauss checked his watch again. "One minute!"

Strauss led Ivanova toward the platform. Before they reached it, the platform began to rise. Something on the outside was trying to get in. Strauss pulled the pin on his last grenade and lobbed it onto the rising platform. They waited in silence.

After the explosion, Strauss reactivated the platform. When the gore-spattered platform reached the floor, the pair stepped on it, Strauss activated the panel, and the two rose toward the ceiling.

The platform led to the surface of the black circular disk. The scattered remains of Soviet and German soldiers littered the ground. They must have surrounded the disk the moment they'd sensed trouble.

Strauss looked at Ivanova. "We're out of time. We need to go."

Ivanova nodded.

After two minutes, they were climbing out of the crater. There were still no signs of artillery.

"Why didn't your people blow this place sky-high?" Strauss said.

"I don't know. This makes no sense."

As they hiked down the knoll, hundreds of soldiers and dozens of T-34s cordoned off the area.

"What the...?" Strauss said.

"Hände hoch!" A Soviet soldier pointed his rifle at Strauss.

Strauss raised his hands in the air. "What the hell's going on, Major?"

"I don't know. I'll get to the bottom of this. Don't worry. I will provide a full report of your bravery to STAVKA."

Ivanova faced the soldier and said something in Russian.

The soldier stared at her for several seconds. His eyes lit up. He then jabbered away excitedly.

"What's he saying?"

"He's praising me for my actions at the Red October Steel Works and telling me it's an honor to meet a Hero of the Soviet Union."

The mention of the Red October Steel Works brought back a torrent of horrific memories. Vivid images of Heinz's lifeless form. Blood on the streets. The desperate desire for oblivion's sweat release. Strauss fought against the crushing weight of his sorrow.

He inclined his head toward Ivanova as tears trickled down his cheeks. "I...I was also at the Red October Steel Works. So...so was my brother. They say a sniper killed him there. A female sniper."

Ivanova glanced away from Strauss, and then regarded him again with her deep blue eyes. "Please, call me Anna." For an instant, she avoided Strauss's gaze. "I was the only female sniper assigned there. I'm sorry. War makes us all do cruel things."

Strauss nodded as he wiped his cheeks with his hand.

The man led Strauss and Ivanova down the hill toward a command tent nestled near the old Tiger tank. As they ventured down the hill, they passed a number of high-ranking Soviet officers. Anna seemed troubled.

"What is it?" Strauss asked.

"I've never seen so many senior officers in one place. Something's not right."

Anna asked their escort a question in Russian. She seemed disturbed by his answer. She turned to Strauss. "He's taking us to see Marshal Zhukov."

Even Strauss recognized the man's name. Zhukov had won the First Order of Suvorov for his actions in the defense of Stalingrad and had attained the rank of Marshal of the Soviet Union.

Why is he here and not focused on tasks more central to the Soviet war effort?

The three entered Zhukov's command tent. Both Anna and the Soviet soldier snapped to attention and saluted the marshal.

Zhukov barked an order in Russian. The two soldiers relaxed their ramrod postures. He motioned to the escort, addressing him in Russian. The man saluted and grabbed Strauss by the shoulder. As the soldier ushered him out of the tent, Strauss heard the marshal interrogating Anna.

∾

Zhukov's henchman loaded Strauss into a truck and transported him to a ramshackle internment camp bristling with razor-sharp concertina wire and populated with gaunt and desperate men.

The camp reeked of stale sweat, urine, feces, gangrene, and trench rot. Roiling waves of rampant vermin scurried about the camp like a living carpet. The flies swarmed so thick they became a second skin for many prisoners. Most men had white flakes infesting their body hair since the Soviets had never bothered to delouse them.

For several hours, Strauss traded stories with the German POWs. Most hadn't eaten since their capture. The Soviets denied medical treatment, starved them, and rationed water to reduce their numbers. Few men survived longer than a week and the NKVD machine-gunned anyone attempting escape.

"Strauss!" a surly male voice called from the camp perimeter.

Strauss shuffled forward, uncertain.

"Strauss?" A massive ursine guard glared at him.

Strauss nodded. The man peeled back a strand of wire so Strauss could exit. With regret, Strauss took one last look back at his countrymen. He wished he could help them, but for all he knew, the Soviets were going to put a bullet in his brain. Those he left behind watched him, their expressions a mixture of pity and longing.

The guard led him to a ditch overflowing with the dead.

A hand tapped his shoulder from behind. Then a familiar voice spoke. "Strauss, I'm glad they didn't shoot you yet."

Strauss turned and trembled with the relief of a man who was only moments earlier certain of death. "Anna, it's good to see you again."

Anna's face was impassive. Her gaze flickered from left to right, betraying a need for secrecy. "Boris, that will be all," she told the guard. "I'll take things from here."

The man saluted and left.

"Come." Anna pointed to an empty, American-supplied Jeep.

Strauss entered the vehicle, and Anna drove away from the camp. "If you try anything, I will shoot you."

Strauss laughed.

Anna showed a fleeting smirk. "They want us both alive."

"Why wouldn't they want *you* alive? Why aren't they going to shoot me?"

"STAVKA knew what was at Kursk Crater. By killing that creature, you disrupted a long-standing arrangement that could have ended the war sooner. My status as a Hero of the Soviet Union and our use as bargaining chips are the only things that saved us. Zhukov worried my execution would harm morale. He also wants to deliver us alive to those things to make amends for the incident. Otherwise, we'd both be dead."

"Wait, what long-standing arrangement?"

"Over ten years ago, my government started a classified program to develop technologies essential for manned space exploration. It had several early successes, most notably the launch of a liquid-fueled rocket.

"Traitors infested the program. They had to be eliminated, which set it back several years. Recent Nazi advancements in rocketry also worried my leaders, especially since they suspect your scientists are working on a wonder weapon—a pilotless flying bomb. That's when these extraterrestrials arrived and offered my leaders a proposal."

"Stalin made a pact with these creatures?" Strauss said, alarmed.

"In a way. In exchange for their technology, my leaders allow them to experiment on our dead, and in limited cases, on our living. My compatriots also encouraged the extraterrestrials to do the same to any fascists found within our borders."

"What are they?"

"They're beings from beyond our solar system who've been observing us for decades. Marshal Zhukov revealed nothing more."

Two weeks ago, Strauss would have considered Anna's tale the ravings of a lunatic. Not anymore. "So, what's next?"

"I am to escort you to Moscow, where I will serve in the Kremlin and you will languish in Lubyanka prison."

Strauss had heard bad things and worse about Lubyanka. After what he'd sacrificed to save Anna, he expected more from her. He thought they'd had a connection. Instead, he directed his thoughts on generating an escape plan. At some point, he'd find a way to ditch Anna. But for now, he played along. "Moscow it is, then."

Anna grinned. "I have no intention of going to Moscow. I shot my escorts before I rescued you. My cousin in the Ukraine will smuggle us out of Soviet territory. Rumor has it the Americans are also interested in space travel."

Strauss smiled. He had never been happier to be wrong about someone in his life.

END

Afterword

I have always been fascinated by the titanic struggle between Germany and the Soviet Union during the Second World War. Surprisingly, most Americans have no idea how critical the Russo-German conflict was in determining that war's ultimate outcome.

This story takes place following the Battle of Kursk, the largest tank battle in human history. While the more familiar Battle of Stalingrad was a key turning point in the war, it was the Battle of Kursk in July 1943 that finally broke the back of the German war machine.

I first became intrigued with the Russo-German conflict when I was a Stanford undergraduate, where I focused on modern European history. The scale of that struggle dwarfed the size of military operations on the Western front by orders of magnitude. It involved a clash between two regimes that had each engaged in genocidal campaigns against both their own people and their subjugated populations. Both governments pressed good people into service, forcing these individuals into situations where there were few or no good choices. It is in such murky conditions where the ingredients for great conflict lie.

When I was a second lieutenant at the Armor Officer Basic Course at Fort Knox, Kentucky, I conducted an in-depth battlefield analysis of the Battle of Kursk. During that exercise, I learned some fascinating facts about the battle. For instance, navigation was difficult at Kursk since the region's high iron deposits generated magnetic fields that rendered magnetic compasses unreliable. I also discovered that the Germans favored the distribution of "wonder drugs" like Pervitin to enhance human performance in tough conditions, particularly on the Eastern Front where the Soviets outnumbered the Germans. I find these small details make a battle seem much more tangible, breathing life into the narrative. Moreover, when a government is willing to distribute methamphetamine to its soldiers to gain an edge, the stakes tend to be existential – and in the Second World War, they were.

Given the willingness of both sides to use any means necessary to win the war, it wasn't hard to imagine what the Soviets might do if they had the opportunity to make a deal with an advanced extraterrestrial civilization. Trading Soviet and German war dead and German POWs to extraterrestrials in exchange for a technological edge would likely have been a small price to pay in Stalin's calculus. Envisioning how such a trade might play out and exploring how it could easily spiral out of control fascinated me. In fact, the premise intrigued me so much that I wrote a novel – my first – based on this short story in late 2013, which advanced in the 2014 Amazon Breakthrough Novel Award Contest.

Besides the historical backdrop, this story is a classic case of opposites attracting. Adding to the tension is the fact that Ivanova and Strauss represent two nations that are bitter enemies, which, incidentally, inspired the title, "Enemy Allies". Strauss is an introverted and highly competent soldier just trying to survive, while Anna is an extroverted and politically savvy leader in a male-dominated environment. They both rightly conclude that the real threat is non-human, and risk their lives and allegiances to confront that challenge.

A shorter version of this story was first published in Episode Three of *Fictionvale Magazine*. An earlier and longer version of this story won an Honorable Mention in the prestigious Writers of the Future Contest's fourth quarter of 2012. Of all the stories in this anthology, this one is my favorite because it draws from my experience as a cavalry officer and my scholarship on the Second World War's Soviet-German conflict. I hope you found it entertaining.

Entropic Order

A figure shrouded in a threadbare woolen cloak toiled at an oaken desk. The mind-blindness would soon overcome the sentinel, extinguishing all traces of an ancient civilization.

Decaying parchment scrolls lay stacked along shelves arrayed haphazardly on mildewed walls. A solitary candle illuminated a vault of knowledge otherwise entombed in darkness. Menacing animated shadows danced on the water-warped shelves as a light draft made the candle's flame flicker ever so slightly. The shadowy apparitions whispered words of woe, ruin and oblivion.

Only one sentinel endured out of thousands, a prehistoric mechanical guardian that had walked the Earth for eons. It knew only loneliness and despair, but faithfully preserved the legacy of its creators.

Over the ages, the wraiths had drained many of its brethren of their life-sustaining energy. Other sentinels had wasted away, sheared by the slow and persistent sands of geologic time.

&

Captain Hrano Hro-san yearned to return home to his wife and three young children after achieving his dream of becoming the first Radan pilot to travel at relativistic speeds. To earn that privilege, he'd endured trials that had killed most of his competitors.

Using his craft's cerebral tuner and amplifier, Hrano directed his thoughts toward the graviton decelerator. At his current relativistic speed, it would take one full Radan rotation to decelerate to reentry velocity.

He channeled his mind toward his home world's main communications node. *Radan Orbital Platform One, this is Captain Hro-san. Request permission to enter the Daaran system.*

Silence.

He tried transmitting via neutrino pulse. No answer.

He pondered the ramifications of time dilation on him and those he'd left behind. He'd expected them to age decades faster, though the prospect didn't worry him. The average Radan lifespan was nearly a thousand years. He'd see his family again.

To pass time, he watched holographic vid footage of his happiest memory: a family trip to Uhlan Travarz, the solar system's largest mountain. Hranuk, his youngest son, giggled as their sightseeing skimmer circled the peak. Hrano's wife, Hranalla, embraced Hrano as they doted on their children.

Hrano had scaled the mountain alone in his youth, outfitted with only an oxygen rebreather and environmental suit. Many had thought him foolish, because technology had made such adventures pointless. But he had had something to prove.

He'd almost succumbed to exposure, wind gusts, and hypoxia. But that was years ago. He'd brought his family to the mountain to help them understand why he'd risked everything on his climb and how it'd forged his character.

Hrano reluctantly returned to his duties. Still no response from Rada. Tiny cracks in his confidence gave way to a deep sense of foreboding. Against standing orders, he reentered the system.

He noticed his star charts seemed inaccurate, and without Rada's navigational guidance, he had no idea if new asteroid belts or other debris stood between him and his planned vector home. He'd have to do his best.

Fortune favored Hrano, until he discovered why no one had responded to his transmissions.

&

When the signal reached the sentinel, its quantum neural network pulsed with possibilities. Was it the one? The neural network calculated the likelihood at sixty-one point eight percent. If it was the Radan who'd disappeared in a pre-fall temporal rift, the probability he would land safely on Earth registered at a dismal five point nine one percent.

The sentinel despaired. The energy wraiths had destroyed the sentinels' Earth-based neutrino transmitters along with the rest of the Radan species, eons ago. The sentinel couldn't use its own transmitters because it lacked spare promethium. Without promethium, the sentinel couldn't activate, though it could hibernate until it received more. When promethium ran low, the sentinels also became more vulnerable to wraith-induced mind-blindness. Even if communication were possible, the dark entities would likely intercept any message.

The sentinel rose on its human-like legs. With the rise of *Homo sapiens*, the sentinels had altered their appearances to avoid detection. This sentinel had filed down its two cranial horns to barely visible stumps. It had done the same to its scales, and had bleached its artificial skin. Yet without access to advanced technology, it appeared as a poor simulacrum of a human being.

Humanity would have destroyed the sentinel long ago if not for its vast knowledge and guidance. But after the Western Roman Empire's collapse, the church needed its help preserving human civilization. The sentinel suspected there were other human cultures on the planet. Yet it had no way of knowing since the last sentinel in the Far East went mind-blind over a millennium ago.

The sentinel awaited the return here, secreted away in the dark bowels of an Italian abbey.

The study's heavy door creaked open. An abbot with a fading widow's peak approached the sentinel. The slight creases on the abbot's face betrayed his late middle age as did his white moustache and beard. He wore an unadorned brown tunic cinched with a thin hemp rope. A small wooden cross dangled from his neck and a woolen cowl covered his head. His eyes sparkled with fierce intellectual intensity.

"We've known each other for years, my dear friend," the abbot said. "I can sense you're getting weaker and it scares me. Civilization is fading. I need your counsel now more than ever."

"All civilizations eventually perish," it replied. "Yet there is much truth in your words."

"I may need your help again before the end," the abbot said, scratching his head. Was he nervous or stressed? Despite millennia of observation, the sentinel still struggled to interpret human behavior. It found embedding sensors in lower life forms a more effective survival strategy than trusting unpredictable humans.

"The monks are restless." The sentinel's human friend got to his point quickly, which it appreciated. It had learned to ignore the first few sentences humans exchanged, as "small talk" seemed devoid of any useful information.

The abbot continued. "I knew when I became abbot, it would never work. I cannot mold these men's habits into the necessary behaviors required for a great civilization – especially like the elder one you've oft described."

"What would you ask of me, Benedict?"

"I believe the monks will attempt to remove me. I humbly beseech you for your protection."

The sentinel's linguistic algorithm ran millions of computations analyzing every word and phrase Benedict uttered. Its complex quantum neural networks then cross-referenced Benedict's speech patterns against his facial expressions and body language. It further analyzed the modulation of Benedict's voice and the pheromones he emitted. It examined all of this data in the context of the entirety of their interactions, and against the abbey's historical records, generating an appropriate response in one trillionth of a second.

"Benedict, when I last emerged amongst your people, a panic ensued. They mistook me for a demon. Absent your intercession, they would have destroyed me," it warned.

"Yet by the Grace of God, I found and protected you in that cave," Benedict said. "During that time, you shared the wonders and achievements of an ancient race. You also inspired me to lead this abbey, one of the last remnants of enlightenment in this dark age. Now human civilization hangs on a precipice. I need your help to keep me here, doing God's work."

"You know I will always be here for you, Benedict."

"What of the demons?"

"If they destroy me, they will turn their attention on your race, for humanity possesses the seeds of the dying one. There is little harm they can do you now, but once your people learn how to manipulate antimatter, the darkness will be drawn to your race like iron to a lodestone."

"You said 'dying one', as if the elder space-faring race is not yet dead."

"There may yet be a survivor, but I need your help to discover the truth."

℘

As a young man, Benedict had been troubled by the dissonance between Christ's teachings and the behaviors he'd observed around him. After completing his studies, he'd left Rome and a life among the nobility to find his true purpose.

His first encounter with the sentinel had shaken the foundations of his faith. During his travels, he had crossed paths with a monk named Romanus.

Impressed by Benedict's faith, Romanus had urged him to establish a hermitage in Subiaco. Devout in his faith, Benedict had agreed. Unbeknownst to Subiaco's inhabitants, he had begun his three-year sojourn in a small cave below Romanus' monastery. During these years, Benedict's only human contact had occurred at sunrise when Romanus had lowered a basket of food and water to him from the abbey.

One cold December evening, Benedict awoke to find a hooded figure standing above him. He first thought it was Romanus, but as his eyes adjusted to the darkness, he saw an inhuman visage, like a defaced statue of some long-forgotten pagan god.

Benedict trembled then prayed. His prayers grew louder and more frenzied. Then the creature intervened. "Stop."

He ended his prayer. "Are you here to tempt me as Satan tempted Jesus?"

The thing watched him impassively.

"Why don't you speak?"

No response.

Benedict rose, confident that God would protect him, and approached the creature. "What are you?"

It answered in an awkwardly cadenced and monotone voice. "I did not expect to find anyone here. I only wanted to hide from the townspeople."

"But you're a demon," Benedict said. "So why should the townspeople frighten you? They couldn't withstand an angel's might, not even a fallen one's."

"I am no demon, though people often mistake me for one. I am another thing entirely."

"What exactly?"

"I am a being made of metal and other elements. My creators were a race that traveled amongst the heavens from a realm that is close, but from a time that has long since passed."

"Impossible," Benedict interrupted. "There is only one Creator, and He is God."

"Perhaps there is one supreme intelligence that set the universe into motion, but I do not concern myself with such things. The origins of the universe do not change the facts of how I came to be. Organic beings created my mind and imbued energy into this inert metallic body. Touch it yourself, so you may know the truth."

Benedict hesitated. "This is devilry. Demons often begin with lesser temptations to drive men to greater ones. I won't be deceived."

The sentinel approached Benedict and placed its cold mechanical hand against his face. In that instant, he knew the truth.

Over the next two years, the sentinel convinced Benedict that his faith could accommodate the existence of other intelligent life. Using mathematics, it showed that the probability that life would emerge on only one world amongst over several hundred billion trillion stars was remote.

Eventually, he reached an accommodation with the sentinel. Four years before Benedict's birth, the Western Roman Empire had fallen after the Germanic chieftain, Odoacer, had deposed Romulus Augustus, the last of the emperors in the west. Benedict promised the sentinel refuge in return for its help rebuilding civilization from Rome's ashes.

ဆ

Hrano circled his home world, struggling to hold back tears. What used to be a spectacular blue orb filled with sparkling cities was now red, desiccated and blanketed with rust. Its desolate wastes held no trace of his people.

Had his family survived?

He saw the wild and perilous blue world Zada a short distance across the cold gulf of space. It would be his final refuge. He reoriented his craft toward Zada, seeking his civilization's survivors, and with them, salvation.

Hrano would face certain death on the third planet orbiting the sun unless he found his people there. Otherwise, if alien microbes didn't kill him, the large reptilian predators swarming the jungles and swamps would.

ॐ

The sentinel's metallic hand rendered itself into a fine needle extending from its forearm.

"How does it work?" Benedict asked, his quavering voice betraying his skepticism.

"It matters not," the sentinel answered in a clipped monotone. "All you need do is pray. I will handle the rest."

It lifted its needle-arm toward Benedict's temple, and discharged a miniscule lightning bolt. He felt a slight shock.

"You are now ready to face the others. I will be watching and protecting you from a distance."

ॐ

The next several days were uneventful, despite Benedict's earlier suspicions. Benedict felt guilty for thinking so poorly of his brethren. He would have to beseech God for forgiveness.

When he arrived at his evening meal, he assumed his position at the head of the table. Constantinus, one of the younger monks, bowed his head solemnly to each of the senior monks before filling their cups with wine.

Benedict had always admired Constantinus' devotion to duty and considered Constantinus one of the few capable of succeeding him. After serving wine, Constantinus distributed coarse loaves of bread.

While Constantinus seemed his normal self, others appeared distracted or nervous. Typically jovial, Marius conspicuously avoided eye contact with everyone, especially Benedict. Francis normally lived for contentious debates on the works of St. Augustine. Tonight, he was silent. Several monks conversed in hushed whispers.

Benedict surveyed the table, and then reached for his cup. The moment he grasped it and raised it to his lips, all conversations stopped. All eyes were on him.

He stared down into his cup and then chuckled.

His brethren seemed perplexed. Aside from his laughter, the room was quiet. Only Constantinus showed the courage to speak. "Abbot Benedict, pray forgive me, but why are you laughing?"

His laughter slowly subsided as he caught his breath. He set his cup back onto the table with a flourish, and then shook his head in disapproval.

Several monks gasped. Many were quaking. Marius' hand covered his brow in an apparent attempt to avoid Benedict's gaze.

"Something terrible has happened tonight," Benedict said. "I've held countless suppers with you. In all of those fellowships, I never once neglected to offer God a prayer of thanksgiving. Tonight, I nearly consumed my drink without doing so. Yet not a single monk challenged my authority. Not one. We all have failed in our duties. I, in particular, failed to provide a good example. For this, I ask your forgiveness, and the forgiveness of our Almighty Father."

There was a collective sigh as Benedict bowed down his head to pray. When he began his blessing, his cup started to quiver. It began as a barely perceivable resonance. Then the cup's vibration crescendoed.

The spectacle seemed to mesmerize the brethren. Benedict feigned indifference.

The cup pulsated to an ear-splitting pitch. Completing his prayer, he made the Sign of the Cross and the cup shattered in an explosion of glass shards and red wine.

Silence shrouded the room. Again, Constantinus was the first to speak. "W-Would you like another cup of wine, Abbot?"

"Yes, brother. Thank you."

Benedict then addressed his comrades. "Please don't let something like a bursting cup prevent you from enjoying your meals. Come, eat and drink."

Some heeded his words. Others cast furtive glances at his bread.

After Constantinus poured wine into Benedict's new cup, the abbot drank it with alacrity, set it down and then tore a piece off his bread. Before taking a bite, he again offered a blessing.

A stained glass window exploded in a flurry of black wings, feathers, and broken glass as a raven descended upon the monks. The bird darted like an arrow toward Benedict. Snatching the loaf of bread, the raven then flew a crisp circuit around the room before exiting the ruined window.

He glanced at the portion of bread he still held. All eyes focused on him.

Once more, the raven flew into the room and perched on the middle of the table, before reaping Benedict's remaining morsel.

The raven conspicuously nibbled on the bread. After finishing its meal, the bird paraded along the table like some vain peacock before collapsing into violent convulsions.

As the raven's carcass lay on the table, Benedict stared down each of his monks. "Forgiveness is a virtue, and I forgive the men who tried to poison me. It is only by the Grace of God that I remain here amongst you. Yet I realize many of you disapprove of my methods, so I shall withdraw back into my cave to commune with God."

∽

Under cover of darkness, the sentinel and Benedict descended the abbey's outer steps to return to the cave at Subiaco. The sentinel wore a heavy woolen cloak to hide itself from prying eyes.

Benedict clasped the sentinel's arm and motioned for it to stop. He faced his friend and said, "I cannot thank you enough for saving my life, though

I fear I've failed both you and humanity. I cast myself out of the abbey tonight because the others tried to murder me. I'm nothing but a coward."

It considered his words. "You didn't fail. The events they witnessed tonight will only increase your legend's potency. Many will fill the valley below, eager to follow your path. With my guidance, you will be a beacon for order amongst a maelstrom of entropy."

"I again am in your debt," Benedict said. "In return for your help, I feel obligated to aid you in your own time of need. Several days ago, you mentioned a dilemma. Perhaps I can be of service?"

It nodded. "I remember. Unfortunately, this problem is beyond your reckoning."

Benedict persisted. "If I cannot assist you, I can still pray for you. Tell me your problem and I will beseech the help of the Almighty."

It ran the decision algorithms through its quantum neural networks. The results showed with a ninety-nine point nine-five percent probability that telling the abbot about its dilemma would not alter the outcome.

"I wish to send a message to someone in the heavens, but lack the necessary power to send a signal that far," the sentinel explained.

"What sort of message?"

"That he may be the last, but that he is not alone; that I remain here to tell him of his people's fate; that my communion with him would likely be my last before the entropic forces of darkness consume me."

Benedict appeared hesitant then said, "Follow me."

When the two reached the cave, Benedict told the sentinel a story.

"In the sixth year of his reign, the pagan Roman emperor, Constantine, was beset by his enemy Maxentius at the Milvian Bridge. The bridge was a strategically vital waypoint over the Tiber River. The battle's outcome would not only determine Constantine's fate, but also the fate of Roman civilization.

"The day before the battle, a crushing melancholy fell over the emperor and his legions. Rome's famous discipline could do much, but it was unlikely to overcome Maxentius's superior numbers.

"Despairing, Constantine looked to the heavens at midday, where he saw a colossal flaming cross with the words, 'by this sign shall you conquer' emblazoned in unmistakable Greek lettering.

"Constantine interpreted this vision as a favorable omen, so he ordered his legions to display the Chi-Rho – the first two letters of Christ's name – on their battle standards.

"The next day, Maxentius arrayed his forces in a line with their backs against the Tiber River, signaling a refusal to retreat. Seizing the initiative, Constantine ordered his cavalry to charge at the enemy host. What first seemed an act of madness became one of audacity.

"War is more about will than about weapons and warriors. Constantine's unexpected assault annihilated Maxentius's cavalry. Constantine's infantry, spurred by his cavalry's triumph, drove Maxentius's forces into the Tiber.

"The victory was so absolute that Constantine believed it an act of God. Pagan no more, Constantine embraced the teachings of Christ, our Lord."

The sentinel pondered his words. "Tell me more about your Christ."

Benedict smiled. "I'd be happy to, but I don't see how that could help resolve your dilemma unless you accept Him as your Lord and Savior."

"I only ask out of curiosity," it said. "It is not often one individual can have such a profound influence on shaping a culture."

Benedict nodded. "Indeed."

So he told the sentinel of Christ's life, suffering, death, and resurrection in a tale spanning half the evening.

When he finished, the sentinel asked, "So, one man suffered lashing that tore the flesh from his back, hammering of nails into his hands, and then hanging from a wooden crucifix until death, to save the souls of all humanity? One man sacrificed all to save all?"

Benedict nodded. "Yes, God loved humanity so much that He sacrificed His only Son for our salvation."

"And the cruciform, it symbolizes this Christ's sacrifice?"

"That, and so much more."

The sentinel again reflected before it spoke. "Now I know what I must do."

℘

Hrano's craft circled Zada as his quantum computer hummed with calculations. The computer no longer had any records of this world.

He ordered his computer to perform a radiometric dating analysis. It rippled with activity and then projected a number: Sixty-five million.

Impossible, he thought. *Even if I had drifted in space for thousands of years, errant hydrogen atoms should have ground me and my craft into dust.*

Computer, recompute.

The quantum computer buzzed, projecting the same answer.

How's this possible? he wondered. *How could I have been gone for so long? Everyone I've ever known is dead. I'll never know what happened to my family or to my people. All is lost.*

Hrano picked a random point on the planet and issued his final order. *Computer, plot a collision course.*

At that moment, they attacked.

His craft shuddered violently. The brilliant blue planet and the gray satellite orbiting it turned black. His canopy was no longer a window to the cosmos. All he saw now was oblivion.

Struggling to understand what was happening, he countermanded his previous order and instructed the craft to orbit the planet.

Computer, status report.

The quantum computer's response was a choking gurgle. *Energy drain. Light and heat loss. Guidance system failure in five minutes. Life support failure in six minutes.*

Hrano needed to think fast.

Computer, calculate a reentry vector.

ℰↄ

Both man and machine climbed the steep mountain's rocky crags. The moon's waning crescent shined on a crystal-clear night. A biting wind swirled down from the peak, overwhelming Benedict with a bone-cold chill.

Reaching the summit, the sentinel turned to Benedict. "You must follow my instructions for this attempt at communication to succeed."

Benedict nodded.

A small, rectangular indentation appeared on the sentinel's previously smooth left arm. A rod extended out of the groove. The sentinel grabbed the object and handed it to Benedict.

"You will need this artifact to protect me. I do not think they can harm you, but they will destroy me if you fail to act."

"Who?"

"Chaos. They are what lie in the darkness. They rule by ruin and delight in decadence. They are the ancient enemy, as old as the cosmos itself, seeking to impose their own entropic order on the universe."

"Are they a threat to my kind?"

"Perhaps," it answered cryptically. "Though your race is still too primitive for them to harm. It is only when you become capable of reaching the stars that they will become a significant threat."

"How can I defeat them?"

"You cannot. They are entities that can neither be created nor destroyed. But you can keep them at bay with this rod. Just point it in their direction. Remain ever vigilant. Just protect me long enough so I can complete my final act."

"Wait. Your final act?"

"Yes. Your stories about Constantine and Christ have inspired me. I shall sacrifice myself so that another may live."

"No!" Benedict screamed as the sentinel rested its back on the ground. It extended its arms at right angles to its torso, forming a cross.

"And if I fail?" Benedict asked in anguish.

"Have faith."

The sentinel's metallic skin became translucent and radiated a brilliant white light.

ಚಿ

Hrano's quantum computer was down to its last two minutes of power. Blackness choked his vision. Space's bitter chill leached into his bones, as his craft traded heat for the computational energy required for navigation.

Then, as suddenly as the attack had begun, a funnel of darkness swirled away from his vessel and spiraled toward the blue orb below. His vision restored, Hrano saw a radiant white light on the surface, shaped like a massive cruciform.

Computer, head toward that beacon. The ship hurled toward the surface, chasing the darkness.

ಚಿ

The burst of light transformed night into day, nearly blinding Benedict. Monks from the abbey below added to the commotion as they sought to determine its source. The townspeople opened their doors and windows to watch the miracle on the mountaintop.

As he held vigil over the sentinel, a swirling black mass descended upon the mountain like a phantom locust swarm.

Benedict reeled from the massless forms confronting him. The dark ethereal entities expanded and thinned in an apparent attempt to douse the sentinel's light. Benedict sprung into action, aiming the sentinel's rod at the infernal cloud.

The wraiths shrank from the ancient weapon's rays of white light. Yet they persevered, rending into smaller pieces like ghostly shards of shattered crystal suspended in air.

The black shards coalesced around the signal, forming a speckled dome above Benedict. They floated, pregnant with malevolence then attacked.

He waved the rod in one direction after another. Yet some of the dark droplets struck home. After each successful strike, the dazzling light faded ever so slightly and the sentinel howled.

₧⁋

The friction from Zada's atmosphere buffeted Hrano's craft during its rapid descent. As his craft sped through wispy clouds illuminated by the immense cruciform, a solitary peninsula stood juxtaposed against a dark blue sea.

₧⁋

The shards of darkness were too numerous. The sentinel's light was faltering. Soon it would fade forever.

Yet Benedict fought on, despite the seeming futility. He also prayed for God's deliverance.

He struggled until he collapsed and lost consciousness.

₧⁋

Benedict woke floating above his Italian homeland.

Is this Heaven? he wondered.

Not Heaven as you understand it, but a heaven nonetheless, a thought answered.

"Where am I? What happened to my friend?" he asked.

A voice behind him answered, "You're on a ship that sails amongst the stars."

When he looked over his shoulder, he thought he was in Hell. The creature behind him had a red scaly face. It was tall, slender and had two spindly arms. Its skull was much larger and angular than a human's. Its jaundiced serpentine eyes unnerved him, but its ram-like horns disturbed him more. Benedict was certain he was in a demon's presence, so he prayed.

The being reassured him, "Fear not. I'm an ally. You saved the last remaining link to my long-dead race. Without you, I would never have found the sentinel, and my people's fate would have forever been a mystery."

"The sentinel was your friend?"

"I never knew it, but it served my people for millions of years. It also awaited my return, for I am the last. When I die, my race dies with me."

"What's your name?" Benedict asked, his voice wavering.

"I am Hrano Hro-san of Rada, the planet your stargazers call Mars."

"I'm Benedict, and I'm sorry I couldn't save the sentinel."

Hrano shook his head. "You did everything you could. It expended its remaining promethium to send the signal. You defended the sentinel long enough for that signal to reach me. For that, I owe you my life."

"How did you survive for so long?"

Hrano was silent for a moment. "I'm not sure. The sentinel's neural networks suggested a vortex opened in space-time, sending me millions of years into the future."

"Neural networks? Space-time?"

"Neural networks constitute the sentinel's mind. My people constructed the sentinels so we could access a sentinel's memories. This one's memories described a rift that opened and transported me far forward in time."

"I see," Benedict said.

"While I was away, the Koronians destroyed my civilization by preventing my people from using technology. My race had become so dependent on it, that most starved when it stopped working. In a final desperate act, my race had scattered the sentinels throughout the solar system to save our culture."

"Koronians?"

"Koronians are the wraiths that attacked the sentinel. They feed on antimatter."

"Where are they now?"

"They've likely retreated to the shadows. They won't bother your kind until long after you develop trans-atmospheric flight and reach the stars."

"What will you do now?"

"The sentinel's memories suggest your civilization is undergoing significant instability. I hope to pass the lessons of my race on to your species, though I must do so from the shadows. You see, the sentinels once appeared as I do. Humans destroyed many of them out of fear.

"Since I'm made of flesh, I cannot alter my appearance as your sentinel did, so I must remain hidden. Only you can know of my existence."

Benedict contemplated Hrano's words. "I accept your offer. Please, take me home."

℘

Hrano and Benedict carved a tomb for the sentinel into the walls of the Subiaco cave.

"I wish I'd known this sentinel. It's done so much for both our peoples," Hrano said.

"I will sorely miss it." Benedict bowed his head in prayer and then looked up at Hrano. "What will become of your spacecraft?"

"It's no longer of use to me. It lacks the power to leave your world, so I will likely jettison it."

Benedict scratched his forehead. "Just how much energy does it have left?"

Hrano crossed his arms. "Roughly enough promethium for several hundred more flights within Earth's atmosphere. Why?"

"Do you have enough to revive the sentinel?"

Hrano's eyes brightened. "You're a wise man. I'm just ashamed I didn't come up with the idea myself."

ဆ

Later that evening, Hrano extracted a hand-sized reddish metal bar from his spacecraft. He opened the sentinel's chest compartment and replaced a dull pink bar with fresh promethium.

Benedict whispered fervent prayers for Hrano's success.

Hrano stepped back from the tomb and waited in silence with Benedict.

The sentinel opened its eyes. "Benedict. It is good to see you again. What took you so long?"

Hrano and Benedict exchanged incredulous glances.

"Your Christ sacrificed himself and then rose from the dead, did he not?" the sentinel asked.

"Yes," Benedict said.

"My survival required that I direct Hrano's ship to me by exhausting my promethium reserves and forcing myself into hibernation. That ship had enough promethium to power ten sentinels. I calculated that one or both of you would reach that solution with a ninety-two point one five percent probability."

Hrano and Benedict burst into laughter.

ဆ

Over the next several decades, Benedict built a network of monasteries that helped shepherd Western culture through the Dark Ages. The Radan and the sentinel counseled Benedict and his successors into the Age of Enlightenment.

Three centuries after the Enlightenment, humanity walked across the moon's surface and planned a manned voyage to Mars powered by the first antimatter drives.

Unbeknownst to humanity, dark and ravenous forces gathered in space's cold abyss.

END

Afterword

I normally plot my stories and then flesh them out during the writing process. This story was different. It stemmed from an experiment in writing via stream of consciousness. I started writing about the sentinel and then started asking myself questions like "what is this thing?", "where is it?", and "why is it here?". I never intended the story to be a tale melding ancient astronauts and advanced artificial intelligence with the hagiography of Saint Benedict and the beginning of the Dark Ages; the characters just took me there.

Writing is a process. I am still experimenting and discovering what works best for me. Whether or not this stream of consciousness produces better fiction than a process involving a detailed outline is something for the reader and posterity to decide.

This story was first published in *Outposts of Beyond*. I hope you enjoyed it.

Jason's Ladders

Wind buffeted the aircraft as it circled chaotically toward a patch of earth on the edge of nowhere. Jason Parker scrambled to find a suitable landing site. The Cessna's instrument panel lights had died, the engine had seized up, and the propeller had puttered out. The plane was losing airspeed fast. Jason shoved the yoke forward, slamming the aircraft's nose toward the ground until the airspeed indicator's needle registered at sixty-eight knots.

He set his radio to the emergency frequency, but his radio was dead. He tried to restart the aircraft in flight, but that failed too. He braced for a hard landing.

Sweat dripped from Jason's brow as he scanned the desert below for a stretch of flat ground amidst a patchwork of yucca and Joshua trees. The aircraft's power loss had been so sudden that it reminded him of what might happen if the machine had experienced an electromagnetic pulse. The Cessna had lost power the instant Jason observed a solid black object on the surface several miles ahead of his flight path. The air around it shimmered like the heat off hot asphalt. Light bent around the object like mirrors in a funhouse, warping and distorting the appearance of the surrounding landscape.

Jason was beginning to regret taking this trip. He especially chided himself for flying solo. Not smart. He could already picture the headlines: "Internet Millionaire Crashes Cessna in Mojave Desert." No. He had to focus on something concrete to stave off the panic threatening to overwhelm him.

Reciting the Cessna's emergency landing procedures kept him calm and alert – for now.

Frantic, Jason scanned the clear blue horizon for a lifeline. His heart rate was elevated. After several tense minutes of searching, he spotted an unpaved dirt road crisscrossing the desert moonscape. It wasn't perfect. Hell, it wasn't even good, but it would have to do.

Jason made his final approach as the ground rushed up to meet him. He took in every rock and ripple on the surface as he drew closer to the landing site. He raised the aircraft's flaps using their wind resistance to slow the plane. A strong crosswind battered the Cessna as Jason fought the controls to keep the wings level with the ground. "Wings level, wings level, wings level," he whispered.

The aircraft wobbled and rattled as its wheels bounced off the desert's rough surface. The impact forced Jason's head forward, smashing his face against the yoke. Jason's teeth clamped down on his tongue, flooding his taste buds with the salty tang of his own blood.

A cloud of dust blanketed the aircraft as it careened down the old dirt road and ground to a halt. Jason wiped sand and blood off his face, unbuckled his seat belt, and stumbled away from the wreck.

It took Jason several minutes to regain his composure. Moments earlier, he'd been fighting for his life. Jason took a few deep breaths before he assessed his situation. He was thankful he didn't have any broken bones. Then the unrelenting desert heat reminded Jason of the next threat to his survival: no water.

He pulled out his smartphone to call for help. *Damn. Batteries are dead.* "Son of a bitch," he yelled as he chucked his phone into the desert.

The Mojave Desert's oppressive heat felt like a hairdryer blowing on Jason's face. His sweat evaporated the instant it escaped his pores. *How the hell can anyone live out here?* he thought. *Nothing for miles with temperatures over one-hundred and twenty degrees Fahrenheit.*

The day hadn't started so badly. The clear July sky had augured a relaxing and peaceful day away from the insanity of Advertech. Since taking his company public seven years ago, Jason felt he had little control of his life. Regulators sniffed into every facet of his business. His investors scrutinized his every move especially when Advertech's share price moved more than five percent. In today's frenetic market, the stock's price moved by more than that almost daily. Whiney employees forced Jason to waste his valuable time trying to retain them by accommodating their demands for perks and absurd job titles. They also complained about the share price any time it was down five percent.

Some days a trip to Vegas was just what the doctor ordered. Flying himself there in his single-engine Cessna was just icing on the cake. Others were victims of fate, but Jason Parker made his own luck. He wasn't someone who needed others; others needed him.

Sometimes he wondered what Tanya was doing these days. He hadn't seen her since that fateful moment at Half Moon Bay thirteen years ago. He hoped she was well. He still had her number, but calling her would only bring back the guilt he felt for leaving her.

Jason turned his attention to more immediate concerns. As he trudged toward Interstate 15, the main freeway between Las Vegas and Los Angeles, he couldn't get that black object out of his mind. It intrigued him and seemed so out of place here. No. Without water he couldn't waste time chasing flights of fancy.

He meandered through the sand for more than an hour. His feet throbbed. He had dressed for a night on the town, not a hike through the desert. He'd have blisters for sure. His throat was parched, his head ached, and his skin was cool to the touch. He recognized the signs of heat exhaustion. He was doomed if he didn't find water soon.

Near midday, Jason observed the same black shape he'd seen from sky, resting on the edge of the horizon. Curious, he made his way toward it. As he drew closer, the object resolved into a ten-foot square cube that warped light.

Despite his extreme thirst, Jason was mesmerized. As he drew closer, the sun's path toward the western horizon quickened. Within an hour, it was twilight. In minutes, it was morning. In seconds, it was sunset. The sun traced an arc across the sky as if Apollo's chariot danced along the heavens.

The cube was now inches from his hands. Tentatively, he reached toward it. The instant his fingers scratched its obsidian surface, Jason found himself elsewhere, nowhere, and everywhere at once. He stood alone, bathed in white. He noticed he was no longer thirsty. An intersection of three blue ladders extended vertically, horizontally, and forward and behind him. Though one of the ladders extended below him, he could see no opening on the white surface upon which he stood. There were no visible walls, ceiling, or floor. All three ladders extended infinitely in all six directions. A tiny gray cube the thickness of a TV remote floated several feet in front of him. Miniscule red buttons embossed all six of its faces.

Jason grabbed the device. He felt an intense shock as fractals of electricity sparked and crackled around him. His ears popped and he was overcome with dizziness. He felt a bump on his left palm. When he looked down at his left hand, a red button was centered there. The gray device had become a part of him.

The white space was an impossible juxtaposition of confinement and liberation. The pervasive whiteness portended everything and nothing. Memory and oblivion. Order and entropy.

Ever the Internet entrepreneur, Jason could not sit by and let fate take control. He made his own luck. In the fast-moving startup world when the situation was uncertain, winners acted. Hesitation killed companies.

Jason strode toward the three-ladder intersection. Gripping the vertical ladder, he began his ascent. He climbed for nearly an hour, yet the ladder never seemed to end. When Jason looked up, he saw more rungs extending into eternity. When Jason glanced down, he could barely see the three-ladder junction. The other two ladders appeared as two-dimensional lines extending forever in each direction.

Absent any better ideas, Jason pressed the button on his left palm.

∞

Jason sat behind a dark oak desk at the far end of a large office. A massive boardroom table dominated the room's center. The office had windows facing what his new memories told him was the Potomac River. Decorating his wall was the photo of the current president, Bryce Thomas. Mountains of snow lined the Potomac's banks, and white flakes drifted lazily into the icy river. Jason wore a dark blue suit with violet power tie and horn-rimmed glasses to correct age-related myopia. His lifetime of new memories at once seemed both bizarre and familiar.

A light source from the center of the boardroom table projected holographic images of the administration's other cabinet officials. Moments later, a three-dimensional image of the man Jason recognized as President Thomas materialized among the other holograms.

"I called this meeting to discuss contingencies to combat our country's current hyperinflation. The Fed has been tightening its monetary policy for the past two months by raising the discount rate to twenty percent. The consensus among economists is that the Fed's actions will force the United States into another Great Depression.

"I cannot allow the current situation to stand. With the dollar depreciating at its current rate, economic planning has become impossible for our government, for businesses, and for American families. While inflation has helped us retire nearly all of our national debt, it has threatened our currency's stability. I fear a volatile currency will lead to an unstable country. Today, I am considering more radical action – namely the retirement of the American dollar and the adoption of a new currency."

Several audible gasps underscored what the president's cabinet officials thought of his proposal. Manuel Hinojosa, the balding Treasury Secretary spoke first. "Mr. President, the course of action you are recommending seems extreme. Despite a quarter century of a weak economy and persistently high unemployment, the dollar has remained the world's reserve currency. The Euro challenged this position and failed; the yuan also nearly supplanted the dollar, but ultimately collapsed. If we disband the dollar, it will threaten the integrity of the global financial system.

"Global stock markets could crash if you even hinted at such an extreme remedy. Instead, I recommend that the government institute temporary price controls for key consumer staples. This solution would also be radical, but not nearly as dire as the actions you're proposing. We can gradually lift these controls as prices moderate and the economy stabilizes."

Jason supported Hinojosa's objection. "Mr. President, I agree with Secretary Hinojosa. If we disbanded the dollar, there would be chaos. Before you'd even announce this policy, you'd have to invoke Executive Directive 51 to circumvent provisions associated with the Posse Comitatus Act. It's the only way you can legally use the military to impose law and order domestically. We would also need to federalize all state, local and municipal forces. Preparation for such a wide-ranging deployment would require at least a month of advanced notice. We would need time to redeploy our forces from overseas and mobilize our Guard and Reserve units. Not to mention the problem of paying all these forces in a currency that doesn't yet exist."

The President rolled his eyes. "Ladies and gentlemen, we face an unprecedented and extraordinary set of circumstances requiring bold and innovative strategies. I believe the simplest solution is to hit the reset button on our financial system. People are suffering. We must take immediate action to ease their pain. I don't want to hear excuses about why my plan won't work. I want to hear recommendations for ensuring its success."

The president's hologram regarded Jason. "Secretary Parker, despite your objections, does the Pentagon have a contingency for the scenario you just described?"

"It does," Jason answered. He couldn't believe this was happening. How'd he become such a patsy?

"Good. I want you to start your preparations today. I aim to make an announcement thirty days from now."

The other cabinet members' body language told Jason they thought the president's plan was insane. However, not one raised any other objections. Madness.

"This principals' meeting is adjoined." The president's hologram disappeared.

The remaining holographic images winked out in unison. Jason found himself in the unenviable position of ordering the United States military to institute martial law. Nevertheless, Jason was determined to succeed. He would do as the president commanded. He didn't get to be the Secretary of Defense by disobeying orders. At least he might help minimize the carnage.

Jason gestured and a holographic image of a four-star general appeared above his boardroom table.

"What are your orders, sir?" the salt-and-pepper-haired Chairman of the Joint Chiefs of Staff, General Roberts, asked.

"Execute Operation Geronimo."

"Now I say this with the utmost respect for your position, sir: Are you out of your mind?"

"I'm afraid not. POTUS ordered it despite my strongest objections."

"Sir, we can't do this. It's crazy. It'll be the end of the Republic."

"General, stay in your lane. You don't make policy. Your job is to execute the president's orders. Do your job or I'll find someone else who will."

"Yes, sir." The general's hologram saluted and flickered out.

ʯ

Jason watched the news holocast with revulsion. Soldiers in riot gear stood between the surging crowd and the grocery store. Razor sharp concertina wire coiled around the storefront like metallic vines.

A female correspondent reported on the ongoing bread riots. "Malnourished American children huddled with their parents in the desperate hope of filling their empty stomachs. Thousands of citizens swarmed for advantage, struggling against one another for a better position in a bread line that stretched for miles. Many of them spent the night in the parking lot just to secure a better position in line.

"With a rapidly deteriorating dollar, most Americans have resigned themselves to long queues and short tempers every payday. Instead of relieving the pain of America's current hyperinflation, technology seems to have made it worse."

The camera panned from a line of gaunt children with distended bellies to the grocery store's display window. The price tags beneath canned goods, cereal, and other items were rising in real-time to keep pace with the dollar's depreciation. The camera panned back to the adults who watched in horror as their purchasing power ticked away minute by minute. The store clerk opened the store's glass doors, his eyes wide with fear.

The reporter continued. "Today marks Day Null for the Thomas administration's exchange offer of one American pound for every one-million American dollars. Since labor rates have not moved in tandem with commodity prices, the exchange offer will leave the overwhelming majority of Americans destitute. In tense standoffs like this one around the country, the American government is pitted against hungry citizens desperate for food."

The crowd surged toward the store's narrow opening. An elderly man fell. The crowd trampled over him. A Molotov cocktail shattered against the storefront window setting the building ablaze. More firebombs sailed in its wake. The crowd surged forward across broken glass and burning embers in a vast onrush of humanity.

The soldiers fought back against the crowd with vomit-inducing sonic weapons and foam generating barriers. Nevertheless, the weight of the crowd was too powerful to stop. Thousands stampeded on the bodies of their brethren to get to the food. In the end, only machine guns and assault rifles succeeded in turning the tide. The press and onlookers dutifully recorded it all for posterity. In this brave new world, shopping had a body count.

Jason could no longer watch, knowing he'd enabled this and thousands of other displays of violence against the American people. It was too late for him to turn back now. He was a mass murderer. Without a family, no one would miss him. After what he'd done, no one would remember him except in anger and hatred. Hell, they'd probably celebrate his death. He opened his desk drawer and stared at the early twenty-first century Glock resting there. After several minutes, he slammed the drawer shut. He just couldn't bring himself to do it.

წ

Jason reappeared before the junction of ladders. Memories of his dark future were vivid and raw. He was young again and the red button fused into his flesh had reappeared.

His curiosity no longer drove him. His last experience had traumatized him enough that he wanted out of this tortured place. His future haunted him. Would he truly become that wretched, pliant and callous stooge? Would he spend his life alone?

If ascending a ladder took him forward in time, Jason reasoned that descending one would send him backward. After climbing down what he arbitrarily decided was an appropriate distance, he activated the red button.

℃

A twenty-three year old Jason stared out into the Pacific Ocean's vastness from his vantage point upon a steep cliff. Seagulls squawked as they dived from a clear azure sky toward the shoreline below. Jason remembered this day well. It was the worst day of his life.

He could hear Tanya's feeble attempt to dam an impending deluge of tears. She approached him gently from behind, testing his tenderness with a tentative touch on his shoulder. He didn't want to push her away, but he had to. How could she be so stubborn? They both had promising futures ahead of them and this one stupid, selfish demand threatened to undo everything.

"I'm so sorry," Tanya pleaded. "We can still make this work. We can see each other twice a year."

"It doesn't matter now. There's only one thing left to do."

"How can you be so clinical about this?" Tanya's mental dam burst and the tears streamed down her cheeks in torrents.

"It's the only way. We're too young to tie ourselves down now. You have a job in D.C. and I'm starting a company in California. Our futures are too bright to throw away on a relationship that might not last."

"Pleeeease!" She sobbed. "We can make it work. I love you so much. How can you be so heartless?"

"I'm not being heartless, just pragmatic. You're not thinking this through. You're being too emotional. My future is here in Silicon Valley, not in Washington, D.C."

Tanya's crying slowly subsided. "Fuck you, you heartless bastard. I don't ever want to speak to you again."

Jason couldn't look at her. Her face only reminded him of how deeply he really did care. "Fine."

ℰℭ

Jason found himself inside the cube again. This time he ascended a ladder to move to the instant before he touched the obsidian artifact. Now that he had established that up transported him forward in time and down took him backward, he started to count each rung of the ladder. Maybe each step represented some discrete unit of time like a year. He counted thirteen rungs to get to his current age and then pressed the red button.

ℰℭ

Jason wore a navy blue business suit. He stood before a simple, two-bedroom house in suburban Virginia. He was twenty-five.

Charlie giggled when his father entered the living room. Tanya gave him a loving hug. After a long week of sales calls, he felt bone tired. He wanted to catch up on some sleep, but he was also excited to see his young family. Despite the low pay and limited control over his schedule, Jason felt content for the first time in his life.

Maybe I'll stay here for a while.

The next several months were blissful. He'd always known there was something missing in his life, but he could never put his finger on it. He'd been alone. There'd been no one with whom to share his successes and failures. The only women he'd seemed to attract as an Internet entrepreneur were more drawn to his money than to him.

He embraced his young wife and son with a yearning for a simpler life. "I love you both so much."

ℰℭ

Jason woke up surrounded by ladders.

His last trip convinced him that the number of ladder rungs he climbed did not correlate to any set amount of time. He now took different approach.

He chose a different ladder. The instant he climbed onto the horizontal ladder and began pulling himself forward, his perspective shifted so he was moving upward. Confused and disoriented, he continued onward. Then he pressed the button.

ဘ

Jason emerged from the cube into a building that looked like a high-tech military installation. The black cube loomed behind him. Red lights blinked around him in sync with an ear-splitting alarm.

A vaguely familiar elderly man sat at a desk at the chamber's opposite end. He recognized Jason. He put his hand on his face in anguish and then regarded Jason, crestfallen.

The man reached below his desk and pulled out an advanced rifle. He aimed it at Jason and put his finger on the trigger. Recognizing danger, Jason leapt back into the dark cube and found himself standing before the cross-ladders again. This time he chose the third ladder, which extended forward and backward. The perspective shifted again as he crawled forward. He counted ten steps and then pressed the button.

ဘ

Jason shuffled forward in a bread line with Tanya and Charlie. He was fifty-seven years old and had difficulty breathing. Hunger pangs wrenched his gut. His new memories comforted him that his thirty-four year old son was there to help him survive.

Jason watched in terror as prices cycled ever upward on foodstuffs secured behind the storefront window. Jason's purchasing power decayed with each passing minute.

Throngs of humanity pressed against one another as the weight of thousands of starving citizens positioned for advantage. Jason's hands shook from a decade of untreated arthritis exacerbated by chronic malnutrition. Tanya was no better. Even his son Charlie looked gaunt and weak from years of famine.

The crowd surged forward when the clerk opened the grocery store's glass doors. Soldiers pushed back, herding the crowd with clear ceramic composite riot shields. Nevertheless, the weight of the hungry human wave was too great for them to hold back. Without any other recourse, the soldiers machine-gunned citizens.

Jason lost his footing. The crowd trampled over his limp body like a force of nature, apathetic to his suffering. Bullets zipped overhead ripping into ready flesh and spraying Jason with blood. A body landed beside him with a wet thud. Charlie. The crowd stampeded over Tanya. Jason's vision faded to black.

℘

The ladders welcomed Jason. Again, he chose another random path. After pressing the button, he found himself standing before a tribunal. A stern Ugandan judge from the International Criminal Court glared at Jason with righteous anger and contempt. "What do you have to say for yourself in answer to your crimes against humanity during the Great Hyperinflation of 2032?"

Jason knew there'd be no mercy. There was no way for him to avoid his fate. They wanted blood. Justice required it. He would hang for his crimes, but deserved worse.

"I have no excuses for my actions. I made bad decisions during a time of tremendous hardship for my nation and its people. I deserve to be treated in the same manner in which I treated them. While I know it will change nothing, I apologize for my actions and regret the decisions I have made."

The jury's verdict was unanimous. Death.

Jason also desired justice for he had experienced his victims' suffering in another life and did not survive the experience. He deserved to suffer and suffer he would.

℘

Jason returned to the ladders after his execution. He chose another path and found himself back in the strange installation where the dark cube resided. This time he did not emerge from the dark cube. He was the old man behind the desk. It was his responsibility to eliminate causality violations. He'd already incinerated two earlier versions of himself today, but now he was wiser. The knowledge of his alternative time lines had made him a better man. His atrocities horrified him. His suffering fortified his resolve.

Blinking red lights and deafening sirens heralded an earlier version of himself. The younger Jason emerged from the cube oblivious to his fate. Jason the elder approached him armed with his plasma rifle.

"Son, you're now a time warden. You are to eliminate all alternative versions of yourself. Don't make the same mistakes I have. I've killed myself over and over for decades. Don't use the rifle. Use your voice. Persuade them all to reenter the cube. Your conscience will be better for it."

The elder Jason handed his incredulous self the plasma rifle and headed for the cube.

"What?" the other Jason asked. It was too late. Jason vanished into the black cube. He now knew what he had to do.

Jason gripped a ladder and climbed for hours until he could no longer see the ladders beneath him. Then he let go and fell into oblivion.

⁎

A younger Jason baked under the Mojave's unrelenting desert sun. A giant black sphere where there was once a dark cube towered over him. Day and night alternated in rapid flashes. Jason left the sphere and headed toward I-15 with several lifetimes of wisdom behind him. He caught a ride to Barstow, found a pay phone, and dialed a phone number he hadn't dialed in thirteen years.

"Hello, Tanya. I hope you're doing well. I miss you and I'd like to start over."

"I miss you too. I also have something to tell you. Something I withheld from you because I didn't want it to ruin your future. Someone here would like to meet you."

"Charlie?" Jason shuddered.

"How did you know?"

END

Afterword

"Jason's Ladders" was inspired by a Robert A. Heinlein short story called ""—And He Built a Crooked House—"", in which an architect builds a house shaped like an unfolded tesseract net. After an earthquake strikes, the tesseract folds into a single cube. When the protagonist enters the house, he finds he cannot escape since all the rooms are connected to one another. Subsequent hijinks ensue.

The concept for this story is very similar, only Jason, the protagonist, discovers a mysterious black cube in the Mojave Desert that distorts space-time. When he touches it, he involuntarily travels through various possibilities in his past and future.

I had fun writing this story, especially imagining the different permutations of Jason's parallel universes and timelines. This story won an Honorable Mention in the prestigious Writers of the Future Contest's second quarter of 2014. I hope you found the story engaging.

Shooting Stars and Schadenfreude

An account by Doctor Maximilian von Borcke

A disconcerting feeling of revulsion overwhelmed me when I touched the strange object, a metallic container the size of a cigar box. Inscribed on it was writing reminiscent of Sumerian cuneiform. The solitary eye engraved on the artifact's face filled me with despair for reasons unknown to my conscious mind.

The weatherworn package had arrived yesterday from St. Petersburg's Mineralogical Museum. I had ripped open the package before reading the attached letter, which was adorned in a script I immediately recognized. Since the war had begun, I'd feared I'd lost contact with my dear friend, Leonid.

My head ached and waves of nausea roiled in my gut. It was only after I returned the container to its package that my queasiness abated. I opened Leonid's letter to learn his reasons for sending me this parcel.

Maximilian,

I wish I were writing you under better circumstances. Tomorrow, I join the Red Army to defend my Motherland against your countrymen. I regret we now find ourselves on opposite sides of this sad struggle. Know that I bear you no ill will. Your politicians are responsible for this fiasco, not you. I still cherish our friendship and scholarly correspondence. It is because of my deep admiration for you that I've sent you this package.

I implore you not to open it until you've read these words. Some things are best left undisturbed.

I shuddered. What horrors had I unleashed?

The artifact is of extraterrestrial origin. I discovered it in September 1908, during an expedition to Siberia's Tunguska region. I found it amidst the destruction wrought by a meteorite that had laid waste to wide swaths of Siberian taiga. I passed the object along to my commander, and it ultimately made its way to the Tsar's court in St. Petersburg.

The impact zone stretched for thousands of versts. There, we discovered queer metallic shards composed of elements unclassifiable on Mendeleev's periodic table. We hauled samples to St. Petersburg for further examination.

I felt betrayed. I had accompanied Leonid on his "second" expedition to the Tunguska impact site in 1927. His first survey had supposedly been in 1921. Both lies.

The sensitive nature of our find led the Tsar to declare this expedition and one that followed secret. In 1914, one of the Tsar's ministers ordered the second excursion to Tunguska. Our mission was to wipe the area clean of all extraterrestrial material.

I had always wondered why we hadn't found any cosmic debris.

The Tungus peasants nearest the site were listless, pale, sickly, and seemingly soulless. Those some distance from the impact reported an eerie green fog that drove men mad. It's difficult to put much stock into these stories, yet so many witnesses reported the same phenomena that they're difficult to ignore. Most believe the metallic fragments were the cause. For humanity's greater good, we collected them and transported them for burial in the bogs beyond St. Petersburg.

After the Revolution, the Soviets engaged in a deception campaign to dissuade other nations from exploring the Tunguska mystery. They sponsored my "initial" survey and the subsequent expedition open to outsiders like you. Forgive me for my dishonesty. I hope you understand my reasons for it given the delicate nature of these disturbing revelations.

I found Leonid's tale to be both outrageous and intriguing. If his claims were true, I had in my possession an artifact of an advanced interstellar civilization. I read further, keen on divining Leonid's purpose in placing this scientific wonder into my humble hands.

I sent you this relic because I trust your judgment. It has the potential to topple nations. Ignorance of its power poses a grave threat to humanity. I ask that you pass it on to scientists in America, as that nation is currently uninvolved in this wasteful European conflict. I trust they will safeguard it until the war ends.

To better times,

Leonid

My friend's trust and my love for the Fatherland resulted in competing loyalties. I held the key to what could end years of bloodshed. Yet it was my friend's confidence in me that placed it into my possession. I pondered for days about what to do. In the end, duty dictated my actions.

ᘓ

In late September 1941, the Führer honored me with a visit to my private estate in Pomerania. I congratulated him on his unbroken string of victories in Soviet Russia and pledged my loyalty to the Nazi regime.

He inquired about the strange item I obtained. I warned him not to touch to it. He thanked me for my concern and we proceeded to examine the object with gloved hands.

Herr Hitler's face became very animated upon observing the relic, while I related its unsettling history. Our meeting ended well. He took the object into his care to pass it on to his scientists for further study. I thanked him and told him I was honored to serve the Fatherland.

ᘓ

In early 1942, I received a second letter. Leonid's writing was barely recognizable, scrawled in weak lettering on filthy smoke-stained paper.

Maximilian,

I received your last letter. Worry not. Your betrayal did not surprise me. I counted on it. As I sit here in this decrepit POW camp and suffer from typhus, your words bring me hope.

You see, I deliberately concealed certain circumstances surrounding the artifact's history. After it reached the Tsar's ministers, a mystic in the Tsar's court came to possess it. Shortly thereafter, Rasputin's influence among the Tsar's family reached heights matched only by his madness.

My claim that this accursed thing could destroy nations was no exaggeration. What I failed to mention is that it destroys them from the inside out rather than from the outside in. Now, it is in your leader's possession.

Long live Mother Russia!

Leonid Kulik

Thus, Leonid's shooting star became the source of my nation's sorrow.

END

Afterword

"Shooting Stars and Schadenfreude" was the first science fiction story I wrote using a first person narrative. It was first published in the *Mad Scientist Journal*. At the time I wrote this piece, I had just discovered H.P. Lovecraft's fiction, and was enamored with his unique story-telling style, which blended science fiction and cosmic horror. I attempted to apply some elements of Lovecraft's style to this story without his notorious purple prose. More specifically, I used the correspondence between Kulik and von Borcke as a device to piece together the story's narrative – a style Lovecraft used in his stories.

In "Shooting Stars and Schadenfreude", I also wanted to meld alternative history with science fiction by spinning a tale about the infamous 1908 Tunguska meteoroid impact. The antagonist, Leonid Kulik, was a real historical figure that led both the 1921 and 1927 expeditions to the Siberian impact site. According to historical accounts, the impact destroyed eight hundred square miles of forest and uprooted eighty million trees. The energy of the blast was roughly one thousand times more powerful than the atomic bomb dropped on Hiroshima. As such, this historic event provided a lot of raw material for me to create an imaginative tale.

By linking Rasputin's troubled history and madness to a cursed alien artifact discovered at Tunguska, I created a situation where Kulik used his friend's disloyalty to get the object into Adolf Hitler's hands. In the end, I hope I produced an interesting and satisfying tale.

Cerebral Vortex

The hollow-skulled dolphin carcasses started washing ashore about a week ago. No matter how many times Dr. Janet Kimball examined the bodies, she was at a loss as to what was behind these mutilations. Dr. Kimball observed an atrocity that had become so common she was almost numb to it – almost, if not for the dolphins' missing gray matter. In all her forty years, she'd never come across such a peculiar and gruesome sight.

This isn't right, she thought. *There aren't any signs of a typical beaching. Normally, the pod would have some survivors.*

The carcasses were in an advanced state of putrefaction. The discolored bodies had bloated abdomens, swollen from what appeared to be a two-week accumulation of gasses in their viscera. The wave action of the tide only added to the miasma choking the shoreline, mixing the salty tang of seawater with the ripeness of decaying flesh. The sight of seagulls engorging themselves on dolphin remains only reaffirmed that nature was a harsh mistress.

Perhaps the military had something to do with the dolphins' beaching, Dr. Kimball surmised. *Maybe the Navy's been conducting war games over the past few weeks. After all, sonar can disorient a dolphin's echolocation system. But that still wouldn't explain the missing gray matter. It just doesn't make any sense.*

The overcast December sky and biting coastal winds were a physical manifestation of her inner gloom. The stench of rot assailed Dr. Kimball's senses. It required all her willpower to avoid vomiting again on the beach, and her surgical mask afforded her nose little protection. She shuffled her sensible, wide-heeled shoes through the sand, and nervously scratched her short, mousey-brown hair.

As a professor in marine sciences and ecological physiology at Stanford's Hopkins Marine Station, Dr. Kimball was one of the most qualified people on the planet to solve this mystery. Yet she struggled to develop a suitable hypothesis to explain what was happening.

Dr. George Mason, the grandfatherly director of Hopkins Marine Station, ambled toward Dr. Kimball as she carefully inspected a dolphin's empty skull cavity with her latex-gloved hands.

"Anything new?" Mason asked, eyes watering as he held the back of his forearm against the surgical mask covering his mouth in a futile attempt to avoid smelling the rank odor that overwhelmed him.

"Unfortunately, no. I'm seeing the same surgical excisions I found in the last pod that washed ashore. The entry wounds also seem to have been cauterized by intense heat," Dr. Kimball explained.

"So what you're telling me is that we have some form of aquatic cattle mutilation?" Mason teased and chuckled at his attempted levity. He then abruptly dry-heaved after inhaling too much putrid air.

Dr. Kimball didn't laugh. "George, whoever is doing this is incredibly sick and twisted. I've never seen anything like it."

She didn't intend to dismiss Mason's jokes. Lord knows she needed a break from the stress. George meant well. In fact, she owed her professional career to Mason.

When she was an undergraduate at Stanford, he had taken an interest in mentoring her. When she struggled in her physiology classes to overcome her squeamishness about dissection, Mason was there to offer encouragement. He convinced her to pursue a PhD in marine sciences and ecological physiology, instead of becoming a medical doctor. When many of Mason's colleagues confused Janet Kimball's dissection-table queasiness for unsuitability in their field, Mason defended her to the last. Without his support, she probably would have returned to her small hometown in Iowa, far away from the bleeding edge of scientific research.

"You still think this is some military conspiracy, don't you?" Mason chortled, and then hacked.

"Of course not. I never did. I just don't think it's a coincidence there's been a ton of military activity off the coast these past few nights."

"The Coast Guard confirmed minimal sonar use in these waters these past few weeks, right?" Mason inquired, adjusting his horn-rimmed spectacles.

"That's true. I just don't think they're telling us the full story. There's something really warped going on here, George, and I don't like it one bit."

"Well, next week the pleasure will be all yours if dolphins keep beaching with their brain boxes missing," Mason ribbed Dr. Kimball. "On Monday, I'm flying to Los Angeles for my cruise to Hawaii. I never had a honeymoon. If I cancel me and my wife's vacation, I do believe my twenty-fifth wedding anniversary may be my last."

A series of flashes from the bluffs surrounding the beach startled Dr. Kimball.

Mason inclined his head toward the uninvited photographers. "Well, we better wrap up fast and call the folks from the lab to get these bodies out of here. Looks like the press is starting to take an interest in our work. I'd rather avoid them if possible. Wouldn't you?"

Dr. Kimball nodded.

ະວ

The next morning, Dr. Kimball responded to another pod washing ashore up north on Stinson Beach. After speaking with some of her international colleagues, Dr. Kimball confirmed that the California Coast seemed to be the only region plagued by these incidents. As she crossed the Golden Gate Bridge, she tuned her radio to NPR. With yesterday's unwanted media attention, Dr. Kimball hoped she'd have enough time to examine the bodies before the press arrived.

"The van der Veen party was last seen Saturday embarking from the Tiburon Yacht Club's docks. One friend of billionaire hedge fund manager Charles van der Veen suggested that the social outing was only planned to last the afternoon. This Thursday, the Coast Guard found van der Veen's yacht adrift about a hundred nautical miles off the Pacific Coast," the radio reporter narrated.

"After examining the ship, California State Police found no evidence of foul play. Coast Guard Lieutenant Martin Remus was on the scene when authorities discovered the empty vessel." The female reporter transitioned to Remus' eyewitness report. "When we arrived at the scene, the boat was floating peacefully. I first thought the passengers had abandoned the ship in a hurry, because they left their food and wine undisturbed in the vessel's dining quarters. The engine was also still idling. The odd thing was the life rafts were still in place. Yet there were no signs of a struggle or violence. It was as if the passengers just vanished."

Good, Dr. Kimball thought, *With the press distracted by some missing billionaire playboy, they'd have little time to interfere with her work today.*

After another hour driving along the meandering road to Stinson Beach, Dr. Kimball began what was becoming her daily death march. As she moved amongst the dark echelons of decomposing and fetid dolphin remains, she noticed a black silhouette several hundred yards from her, juxtaposed against the gray fog blanketing the beach. Fog was nothing new to Stinson Beach, but the shadow calmly strolling amongst another massacre disturbed Dr. Kimball. The figure was armed with what appeared to be a rectangular device.

Curious, Dr. Kimball walked cautiously toward the individual. After all, someone who could dispassionately go about his or her business amidst such an atrocity had to be up to something.

As she drew closer, she noticed the figure wore some kind of military uniform.

"Excuse me," she announced. "Do you have any idea what's going on here? Why these dolphins are washing ashore with such regularity?"

"Ah, Dr. Kimball," the man replied. "I figured we'd run into each other sooner or later. I had hoped it would be later rather than sooner. Where's the old man?"

Dr. Kimball failed to conceal her astonishment and dismay. She countered with a disorganized barrage of questions, unable to contain her outrage. "How did you know my name? Why are you here? What the hell are you people up to? Who's experimenting on these dolphins?"

"Now, now, Dr. Kimball. All in due time. We have some questions for you first." The man dismissed her protests with an air of authority.

Before responding, Dr. Kimball paused, breathed deeply, and observed her subject dispassionately like the scientist she was. The man wore two golden oak leaf clusters on his left and right lapels. The black nameplate over his upper right pocket had white lettering bearing the engraved name, "Reynolds". His left breast had a patchwork of colored rectangles and a pin that had two fish or dolphins facing toward each other. Short and stocky with bright red hair, the man seemed oddly nonchalant to Dr. Kimball.

"I refuse to submit to any inquiry until I know who you are, why you're here, and how you know my name," Dr. Kimball fired back.

The man smirked at her comment, and winked at her. He then brazenly pointed the rectangular device in her direction. It reacted with a high-pitched squeal.

"My, my, Dr. Kimball, you've been a busy bee. Your exposure is approaching 5,000 millirems," the man stated matter-of-factly.

"My what?" Dr. Kimball huffed in exasperation.

"Your radiation exposure is about to surpass the maximum annual dose for American nuclear personnel. I suspect the old man would have similar readings. You might want to give him a heads-up."

Reynolds now had Dr. Kimball's undivided attention.

"How in the hell have I been exposed to radiation? What on earth does it have to do with dolphins? And why do you keep calling Dr. Mason 'old man'? Frankly, I find it disrespectful and rude."

"Dr. Kimball, I'm asking the questions here. I'll be happy to answer any questions I'm able to, after I've debriefed you," the cocky redhead declared with a smug, self-satisfied grin.

Dr. Kimball strove to balance her quest for knowledge against her desire for control. "I need some answers now," she declared, refusing to budge.

"OK, fine. Since you've obviously gotten your panties in a bunch, I'll tell you a bit about myself. The name's Reynolds. I'm a Lieutenant Commander in the United States Navy. Like you, the Navy is very interested in learning more about what's happening to these dolphins."

Dr. Kimball had suspected as much, but she allowed the officer to continue without interruption.

"Tell me a little about these dolphins. What subspecies are they? Where do they live? How deep do they dive?"

How deep do they dive? Now there's an odd question.

Dr. Kimball instantly transformed into professor mode. "These animals are known as *Delphinus capensis*, more commonly known as the long-beaked common dolphin. You can tell from their rounded forehead and moderately long beak. They travel in families of ten to thirty individuals, and belong to larger groupings of between one hundred to five hundred animals. They tend to live within fifty to one hundred nautical miles off the coast."

Dr. Kimball deliberately left out the answer to the last question – an omission Reynolds did not miss.

"How deep can they dive?" he repeated with a twinkle in his eyes.

"At least nine hundred feet or so."

"Is it possible for them to venture any deeper than say, two thousand feet?"

"I doubt they could for any extended period of time. Why?"

Reynolds shrugged, and then ignored her question. "Dr. Kimball, in your autopsies, have you ever come across any evidence these dolphins suffered as a result of rapid ascension from extreme depths?"

Now Dr. Kimball was intrigued. The dolphins did indeed show signs of decompression sickness. For instance, many of them had accumulated tiny bubbles beneath their blubber. The greater mystery of the dolphins' missing gray matter had distracted her from this other peculiarity.

"Come to think of it, they did. Why do you ask?"

"I'm sorry, Dr. Kimball, you don't have clearance for that information."

"Are you kidding me? I have a Top Secret clearance," Dr. Kimball argued. "I did some work for the government a few years back that required me to have one."

"I'm sorry, doc, this matter requires a Top Secret SCI clearance, and you don't have one of those. But that's not important right now. I still have more questions."

Janet took a deep breath, and tried to regain her mental composure. "Until you tell me what this is all about, I'm done answering your questions." Dr. Kimball dug in her heels. "Plus, you can't tell somebody they've been exposed to dangerous levels of radiation, and then change the subject. I demand answers."

Reynolds looked at Dr. Kimball, then down at the dolphin carcasses strewn across the beach, then back up at her. "Fair enough," he said, "We believe that whatever's sucking the brains from these dolphins is using tech with a nuclear-powered heating source because the residue on these dolphins is highly radioactive. You probably shouldn't spend any more time around them. In fact, the Navy sent a team to Hopkins Marine Station today to decon your labs, and remove the dolphin remains you've stored there."

"You've no right to do that!" Dr. Kimball protested.

"The hell we don't. The carcasses are all highly radioactive. It's illegal for anyone to have that much radioactive material in a civilian lab without explicit government permission."

"Fine." Dr. Kimball sighed. "By the way, you said, 'whatever is extracting their brains', not whoever. Why?"

"I didn't say that," Reynolds replied. His expression was blank. Then he changed the subject. "I have one more question before I go. How intelligent are dolphins compared to humans?"

By this point, Dr. Kimball was at the end of her rope, but she figured this question was an easy one, so she might as well answer it. "While a dolphin's brain is about twenty-five percent heavier than a human brain, the metric that counts is the encephalization quotient or EQ. EQ measures the ratio of brain size to body size. Humans have an EQ of over seven, while dolphins' EQs range between three and six, depending on the species. In other words, dolphins are second only to humans in terms of intelligence."

"If you had to measure the number of floating point operations a dolphin can process per second, what would that number be?" Reynolds asked.

Dr. Kimball was dumbfounded. "Floating point what?"

"Never mind." Reynolds shrugged. "We appreciate your cooperation, Dr. Kimball."

Reynolds reached into his trouser pocket and handed Dr. Kimball his business card. "If you have any questions or anything peculiar comes up, don't hesitate to call me. And remember, stay away from the dolphins. Your long-term health depends on it."

As Lieutenant Commander Reynolds turned and walked away, he abruptly stopped, looked over his shoulder and said, "Do you know of any scientists doing research on how marine life responds to astronomical events? Like meteorites impacting the ocean, for instance?"

The question was so strange and unexpected that Dr. Kimball just stared blankly at Reynolds for a good ten seconds before she convinced herself the man was actually serious.

"No, Commander Reynolds, I'm fairly certain no one's ever done any such research. Why?"

"No reason. Thanks again for your cooperation."

∞

Two nights later, Dr. Kimball met her boyfriend, Peder, at the upscale Sundance Steakhouse in Palo Alto. Dr. Peder Hermansen was an associate professor in Stanford's computer science department with a promising career in cybernetics. He was tall, thin as a rail, and had pale white skin, blonde hair, and piercing blue eyes.

The couple began the night with the usual flirtatious pleasantries like any new couple. Nevertheless, it wasn't long before Peder detected a strange uneasiness lying just beneath Janet's forced cheerfulness.

"Janet, you seem distracted tonight. What's bothering you?" Peder brushed his hand across her shoulder to show his concern.

"It's what's happening to the dolphins," she lied. She had had plenty of time to fortify herself from that horror.

"You seemed troubled by it the last time we were together, but not this upset. If you don't mind me prying, what is it really?"

"The other day, on Stinson Beach, I came across a naval officer with a Geiger counter. He told me I'd been exposed to close to the maximum annual radiation dose for an American nuclear technician."

"Oh, my God," Peder whispered. "Are you sure he wasn't just lying to you?"

"Yeah, I'm sure. I went to see my physician, who confirmed it."

"Are you going to be all right?"

"The doctor said I'd be fine, as long as I stay away from the dolphins."

"Whoa, wait a second. First, how'd you get exposed to that much radiation? Second, what the heck does it have to do with dolphins?"

An awkward silence shrouded the couple as Janet nervously played with her fork.

"Well, if you'd rather not discuss it, I get it," Peder said sympathetically. "I just wanted to let you know I'm here for you."

"No, I understand your concern. To be honest, I'm just having trouble wrapping my head around some of the questions I was asked. They seemed really odd things for someone to ask a dolphin expert."

"What were they?"

"He wanted to know if the dolphins exhibited any signs of decompression sickness. He also asked me if I knew of any scientists who have studied how meteor showers affect marine life. And then he wanted to know how smart dolphins were as defined by some weird measurement having to do with floating."

Peder laughed.

"What's so funny?" Janet asked, annoyed he didn't seem to be taking her seriously.

Peder held up his open palms in an effort to calm her. "I'm sorry, Janet. I just find the third question amusing, because I think I may be able to answer it."

"What?" Janet was incredulous.

"Your military man wanted to know the processing power of a dolphin's brain. He was referring to a measurement in computer science known as floating-point operations per second, or flops. While I couldn't tell you what the average processing power of a dolphin brain is, I could tell you about the human brain."

"Sure, if you wouldn't mind."

"Well, you see, the average human brain still has more processing power than the world's most advanced supercomputer. Some experts say the average human brain has nearly a hundred petaflops of computing power, while the world's most advanced supercomputer has just over ten petaflops."

"A peta what?"

"Sorry. A petaflop is about one quadrillion mathematical computations per second."

"Why on earth would he want to know about the processing power of a dolphin's brain?"

"Maybe the military's working on some sort of a biological computing system that harnesses dolphin brain power. You told me once that dolphins use large areas of their brains for echolocation, right? Maybe the Navy is working on an advanced form of sonar."

Janet's mind started racing. *It all made sense. A military observer who knows my full name. Questions on dolphin intelligence, and the depth to which they could dive. Perhaps the Navy does want to harness a biological computer in an advanced submarine, and needs to find a way to neutralize the chemistry causing decompression sickness.*

"The Navy's behind these atrocities," Janet concluded. "Hey, I'm sorry to cut our dinner short, but I need to go to Moffett Field." Janet kissed Peder, and left the restaurant so she could give Lieutenant Commander Reynolds a piece of her mind.

∽

As Dr. Kimball travelled south on Highway 101, she fumed. *How dare they do this to another intelligent species? The sheer arrogance. I'm going to make them pay.*

"We interrupt this program to report breaking news. In the past hour, Santa Cruz residents have reported seeing dozens of bodies washing ashore," the radio reporter announced.

Great, Dr. Kimball thought. *The military is killing more dolphins, and I can't examine them.*

"A total of fifty-four males and twenty-three females washed ashore in what appears to be the worst mass murder in California history. The body of missing billionaire Charles van der Veen was found among the dead. Authorities also believe the victims include the crew of the container ship *Puget*, which was thought lost to pirates some time after it was last seen two weeks ago passing through the Strait of Malacca. Also discovered were several missing passengers from a *Festival* cruise ship that embarked from Los Angeles several days ago. The head of each body was sliced open, and had its brain removed."

Dr. Kimball's Prius swerved toward the shoulder of Highway 101, as she struggled to process what she had just heard.

Her mobile phone buzzed. "What?" she asked the caller. "No, it can't be. That's not possible. I just spoke to him a few days ago."

Dr. Kimball didn't consider herself a religious person, but in her anguish, she raised her eyes to the heavens, and silently asked, "Why?"

She had just gotten an unwanted promotion after authorities had recovered Dr. Mason's brainless body amidst the carnage. Her dear friend and mentor was now gone forever.

೮

After she'd had time to collect herself, Dr. Kimball called Lieutenant Commander Reynolds to schedule a meeting. Dr. Mason's loss rattled her to the core. She vowed to discover what was really going on. Maybe she could help the government prevent more people from being murdered and mutilated.

While the government's extraction of dolphin brains to build a biological computer had seemed plausible to her, kidnapping American citizens to remove their gray matter did not. Something far more sinister was at work.

For convenience, Reynolds agreed to meet her the following day at Lake Lagunita on the Stanford campus. The university hadn't filled the artificial lake since the late nineties. Dr. Kimball and Reynolds both expected the area to be relatively quiet so they could meet discreetly.

"Lieutenant Commander Reynolds, your business card says your first name is John. May I call you John?"

Reynolds nodded.

"John, please tell me what's really going on. I can't take it anymore. First dolphins, now people?"

"Dr. Kimball…"

"Please, call me Janet," Dr. Kimball interrupted.

"Janet, those details are classified. However, I need to ask you a few harmless questions, if you'll indulge me."

"I never get anything but questions and more questions from you. I refuse to answer any more of them," Janet snapped.

"Please, Janet, give me a chance."

"Fine."

"When did the dolphins start beaching?"

"On November third, if I remember correctly."

"You did. Can you remember anything else of note that happened on or about that date?"

"Oh, I don't know. It was a sunny day for all I can remember."

"What about the night before?"

"It was a pleasant night. I remember spending the evening with a friend observing a beautiful meteor shower… Wait, didn't you ask me something about marine life and meteor showers?"

"Indeed."

"You also asked me about the processing capacity of a dolphin's brain."

"Yup."

"Now something is removing human brains."

"With emphasis on the word, 'something'," Reynolds added with a mischievous wink.

"Oh, my God. What can I do to help?"

ⅎ

The Defense Department processed Dr. Kimball's TS/SCI clearance in record time – just under forty-eight hours. Stanford quickly approved her temporary assignment to work on a classified military project.

Dr. Kimball expected her new clearance to provide her with access to untold military secrets. She was quickly disappointed, and expressed as much during her initial briefing from John Reynolds.

The two met shortly after midnight Wednesday morning, so they could discuss classified information without attracting any unwanted attention. Since Janet's office at Moffett Field wasn't ready yet, they again settled on Lake Lagunita for the location.

Dr. Kimball was bundled in a warm hoodie and jeans to keep out the fierce winds swirling throughout the Bay Area. The chill in the air paralleled the darkness unfurling off the Pacific Coast. For the first time, Dr. Kimball saw John Reynolds in civilian clothes. He wore neatly pressed blue jeans and a black leather bomber jacket.

"So, the military knows as much about what's going on as I do," Dr. Kimball lamented.

"That's partly true, Janet. However, you never gave me a chance to brief you on Operation Leviathan."

"Do tell."

"After the meteorite landed about two-hundred and fifty-four nautical miles off the California coast, MASINT from several of our military satellites detected a high level of radiation near the crash site."

"Whoa, whoa. Stop right there. What's 'MASINT'?"

"My apologies, Janet. MASINT is an acronym for measurement and signature intelligence. In the past, we've used it to detect the existence of foreign governments' nuclear programs. We used similar technologies to detect a radiation signature near the impact zone."

"Is this the same radiation signature you detected on the dolphins?" Dr. Kimball inquired.

"Yes. And it was the same one we detected on the human corpses. But that's not what really threw us for a loop."

"Out with it."

"The signature was a radioactive isotope never before observed here on Earth."

Janet's heart skipped a beat. "Well, where's it from?"

"The meteorite, obviously. When the Defense Intelligence Agency detected the radiation signature, the Navy had a *Seawolf* class submarine operating in the vicinity at that time. The submarine, the *USS Connecticut*, investigated the radiation signature at its source. However, the Navy lost contact with the *Connecticut* once the sub came within five nautical miles of its target. We haven't heard from the crew since."

"Hold on a second. Are you telling me that the United States Navy lost a nuclear-powered submarine off the California coast?" Janet asked.

"Janet, I never said that. I only said we lost *contact* with the sub's crew. For all I know, the sub's communications equipment may have been damaged. Alternatively, whatever's out there could be jamming the sub's transmissions."

"I get it," Janet said. "The U.S. Government won't admit publicly that it lost a sub. So what does the military really think is going on?"

"Well, given the strange course of events following the meteorite's arrival, including the surgical removal of brain matter from both man and dolphin, we believe some sort of extraterrestrial intelligence is involved."

"I can't believe I'm saying this, but I think that's the only possible explanation that accounts for everything," Janet agreed. "That's why you were so interested in the processing power of a dolphin's brain, isn't it? The military believes whatever is out there requires more processing power than any of our current technologies, so it's stealing the biological circuitry of the two most intelligent creatures on Earth."

"Unfortunately, Janet, you hit the nail right on the head. Whatever's out there, it's trying to build or repair some sort of advanced biological computer."

"So, how do you plan to end this?"

"That decision is above both our pay grades."

⃝

Shortly after Dr. Kimball's security briefing, another forty human bodies washed ashore off Half Moon Bay. Janet's first official day on the job would be at two a.m. on the beach rather than at the program's makeshift headquarters at Moffett Field.

She passed several bullnecked Marines on her way to the beach, each of them challenging her right to be there. She flashed her security badge at least three times before she arrived at her destination.

The Marines had neatly lined the bodies in tight rows along the beach, and had wrapped them in black body bags. The hasty order the Marines had imposed on the tragedy failed to mask its underlying chaos.

As Dr. Kimball drew closer, John Reynolds signaled her to stop. She complied after noticing five people wearing protective gear and gas masks. Reynolds was clad in a similar suit, but his gas mask was still hanging from his right hip. He walked briskly to Dr. Kimball, and handed her a cellophane package and a gas mask, "Put this on before you get any closer to the bodies."

Dr. Kimball spent twenty minutes with Reynolds, donning her chemical suit, and learning how to form an airtight seal with her gas mask. Once she was ready, Reynolds escorted her to the five others gathered around a victim.

One of the five appeared to be a medical examiner. The examiner knelt before the corpse, scraping tissue samples from its empty cranium with a long cotton swab. With the gas mask securely fastened to her face, Dr. Kimball could smell nothing but rubber.

The body lying before her was that of an unclothed and slender adult female. Her face had a closed mouth and blank stare. The dead woman's skin was swollen and wrinkled after several days in the Pacific. The inside of the woman's cranium was stripped to the bone.

The medical examiner looked up at Dr. Kimball, and asked her several questions regarding the similarities between the humans' and dolphins' wounds.

They were virtually identical.

If she could have smelled their rotting flesh, Dr. Kimball would have emptied her stomach. Examining the mutilated skulls of dolphins was one thing. Witnessing a similar atrocity against humanity was entirely another.

She couldn't help but imagine a vast alien intelligence imposing its will on the planet's most dominant species like a man would on cattle – extracting the most useful parts, and discarding the rest. In her mind's eye, she saw a living and throbbing human brain network powering an extraterrestrial bio-computer. Did these minds remain sentient, serving as slaves to a predatory species? Did they suffer?

୫୦

A week later, dead children started washing ashore. While sharing lunch with Janet at Stanford's Tressider Memorial Union, Peder argued that the pattern seemed to follow increasingly higher processing capacity.

"You see," Peder pointed out. "By the time children are about three years old, the brain has formed about one quadrillion connections, which is double that of the average adult. At around eleven years old, the brain begins pruning unused connections."

"So a child would have about double the processing capacity of an adult?" Janet clarified.

"That's right."

The implications of Peder's response horrified Janet.

℣

Dr. Kimball pulled up to the Moffett Field gate, and flashed her special access badge. She drove to Hangar One, a massive dome-shaped structure towering almost two hundred feet above the joint military-NASA base. The complex covered eight acres – the equivalent of ten football fields.

John Reynold's office was located in a makeshift work area NASA and the military had recently cobbled together. It was a hive of activity, with dozens of scientists and military personnel bustling throughout. LCD monitors lined the hastily assembled walls with images ranging from cable news networks to live satellite feeds of an area about two-hundred and fifty nautical miles off the Pacific Coast.

The moment Dr. Kimball entered Reynolds' office she confronted him. "Please, John, tell me the military is going to do something about this."

"I assure you, we are. The president is busy coordinating with the British, French, Russians, Chinese, Pakistanis, Indians, Israelis, and even the North Koreans as part of a nuclear nonproliferation conference. I think it speaks volumes that no such group has ever before assembled in one place to discuss this topic. I suspect the real reason the president called this meeting was to warn them of an impending ballistic missile launch. He wouldn't want them mistaking it for an incoming U.S. nuclear attack."

"You're kidding me. The United States Government is seriously going to drop nukes off California's coast?" Janet asked in disbelief.

"Janet, I can't confirm or deny that. I know about as much as you do. Plus, what else would you have us do? We can't get within five nautical miles of that subsurface impact crater."

Exasperated, Janet asked, "Hasn't anyone tried communicating with whatever's out there?"

"Of course," Reynolds answered. "You didn't hear this from me, but a few of my friends working at the National Security Agency told me they've been beaming messages toward the impact site for weeks. However, when human bodies started washing up on the coast, the intent of our visitors became abundantly clear. After that, the U.S. military channeled all its resources into a more forceful solution."

"So then what? How is the military going to proceed?"

"Here's how I think it'll play out. This is just my opinion, based on what I know of military strategy. Once the president communicates his intentions to every global nuclear power, he's likely to order a few *Ohio* class ballistic missile submarines to launch several dozen missiles at the impact site. Each missile carries multiple nuclear warheads. I wouldn't be surprised if several submarines are en route as we speak."

"How do you know that?" Janet asked.

"Well, I don't really. However, I'm a submariner, and have lots of Naval Academy classmates in that branch of service. More specifically, I have some friends in Bremerton, Washington who are supposed to be on shore leave. Yet none has returned my calls. Something big's definitely up."

"But wouldn't the jet stream carry nuclear fallout east over the United States?"

"I'm sure the Pentagon's planners would calibrate the missiles so they'd detonate several thousand feet under water. Hopefully that would mitigate any serious fallout," Reynolds speculated.

"God help us if you're right about the government's solution."

ဆ

By the time the Navy's subs traveled from their Bangor pens in Bremerton, Washington to launch points at several remote corners of the Pacific Ocean, the American people had started doubting the government's official cover story. Somehow, the image of a twisted mass murderer rampaging along the California coast, scalping people and removing their brains, no longer seemed credible. The body count was simply too horrific for one demented soul to accomplish alone.

Bringing al Qaeda into the mix as a cover story worked for a while. It both terrified people, and took advantage of their worst impulses.

At some point, though, someone would inevitably start digging further. That someone was no-holds-barred investigative journalist, Kurt Stillwell. Stillwell's claim to notoriety was his exposure of Hollywood sex scandals, allegedly by hacking into victims' cell phones.

Stillwell had been following Dr. Kimball to her strange new Moffett Field office for several days now. The fact that she had been the first scientist to observe and examine the beached and brainless dolphin carcasses had put her onto Stillwell's radar. Her trips to Moffett seemed particularly odd to Stillwell, because she had been promoted to lead Hopkins Marine Station after its former director's untimely demise. Why was she here when she should have been near Monterey Bay?

On her way to her Stanford campus office, Stillwell ambushed Dr. Kimball with his camera operator in tow. "Dr. Kimball, what's it like to work with the government on a top secret project? Why won't you tell the American people why the dolphin and human atrocities are linked?"

"How did you know I'm working with the government?" Dr. Kimball asked, dumbfounded.

The gleam in Stillwell's eyes told Dr. Kimball he hadn't known, but had just thrown the question out there to bait her into unwittingly revealing privileged information. "Dr. Kimball, how long have you been working on this program? How could you let this happen to innocent people?"

The last question struck a nerve, unleashing all the stress and anxiety that Dr. Kimball had been bottling up for so many weeks. Janet lost it. She threw a clumsy right hook at Stillwell, knocking him flat on his backside.

Stillwell quickly jumped back on his feet, and started fiddling with his earpiece. He was anxious to exploit the moment, and prove to his audience that Janet was the willing executioner of a callous government, bent on human experimentation.

Almost simultaneously, the ground began shaking violently, with the seemingly solid asphalt rippling like a wave. Car alarms began blaring throughout campus. Janet noticed nearby buildings shaking ferociously, and stirring up clouds of dust and billows of smoke. The sound of glass shattering inundated her ears. Dr. Kimball was terrified, and it seemed as if the temblor would never end. As the earthquake finally began to subside, there was a bright flash of light on the western horizon.

"Carl, start rolling the camera! Now!" Stillwell ordered his companion. He then began reporting in his best sensational tone. "Our San Francisco affiliate has just reported a massive earthquake about three hundred miles off the California coast. The tremor lasted about three minutes, and was followed by a violent flash of light from beneath the ocean's surface..."

Oh my God, Dr. Kimball thought. *They've actually done it. Those crazy bastards actually fired dozens of multi-megaton nuclear weapons off their own coast. God help us.*

Dr. Kimball braced herself for the inevitable mushroom cloud. It never came. Instead, a massive fireball rocketed toward the heavens.

"...our Washington D.C. affiliate reports that the White House will not comment on the situation. Several prominent military analysts are speculating that the North Koreans may have successfully detonated a nuclear weapon within several hundred miles off the U.S. coast...Wait, this just in. An immense fireball has just emerged from the source of the quake, and is rocketing toward space. Sources are suggesting that there may have been a failed military test off the American coast. Stay tuned for more details on this developing story after a few brief words from our sponsors."

&

Janet's father always used to say, "A good lie finds more believers than a bad truth." Over the next several weeks, the government settled onto a plausible cover story. Janet caught the tail end of the Defense Secretary's press briefing on the news while she was getting ready for work one morning.

"Our test of the next-generation Massive Ordinance Penetrator (MOP) worked better than we'd anticipated," the Secretary of Defense lied, "Our new bunker-busting bomb is capable of penetrating nearly a mile beneath the surface. We believe the device's explosion inadvertently triggered a seismic shock along several San Francisco Bay Area fault lines. The fireball observers reported was an errant submarine-launched cruise missile carrying a MOP. Fortunately, the missile landed harmlessly in the Pacific Ocean."

Janet just shook her head. Her father was a wise man. The public really did seem to prefer the shiny lie to the dark truth.

The world of marine life no longer satisfied Dr. Kimball's scientific curiosity. Her attention was now firmly fixed on the heavens. She believed that whatever had briefly visited Earth would inevitably return, and she wanted humanity to be prepared for the next encounter.

END

Afterword

They say that your muse can be fickle, and you never know when she'll strike you with inspiration. "Cerebral Vortex" is one of those stories that seemed to come to me out of the ether. The story's concept hit me on Veteran's Day weekend in November 2011 while I was driving from my home in the East Bay to see a Forty-Niners football game in San Francisco. The image of lobotomized dolphins washing ashore on Northern California beaches just hit me out of the blue. Deconstructing the mystery of why it was happening became the germ of a story.

While "Cerebral Vortex" was my second serious attempt to write a science fiction short story, it was the first story I submitted to various markets. It was also my first submission to the prestigious Writers of the Future Contest, where it garnered an Honorable Mention in the Contest's first quarter of 2012. That Honorable Mention was the first validation I had ever received for my work, and it encouraged me to continue writing. I ultimately sold the story to *NewMyths.com*, where it appeared in September 2013.

The Witchwood Whispers

The day Karolyn's mother, Tara, succumbed to a foul pox was frigid and dreary. Snow banks as high as cottages loomed over the colony's ice-encrusted cobblestone roads as the starving populace clawed its way out of a wintry oblivion.

Tara's sores had hatched an orgy of writhing olive-colored larvae. Her body had collapsed into a ruin of putrid flesh and brittle bone. Karolyn would remember her mother's stench most: a vile stew of visceral gases and decay melding with the exotic toxins of an infectious parasite. It was a crude concoction of two disparate species, one of which did not belong on this world.

Karolyn's father, Jonas, had buried Tara's broken body on the forest's edge, chiseling a narrow grave in the unyielding frozen soil. By spring, Tara's remains had disappeared, likely carried off by some wild beast during the thaw.

On her deathbed, Tara had entrusted Karolyn, her eldest child, with watching over her two siblings. It was a promise Karolyn had failed to keep.

Autumn had come, and Karolyn's pale-haired sister was gone, probably lost forever. Karolyn searched every crevice in her family's modest thatch-roofed cottage. Her skin glistened with sweat and her fierce blue eyes welled with unshed tears as she trembled under the crushing weight of her failure.

"Gretchen!" Karolyn screamed.

That Gretchen had wandered into the *Wodenwald* – a place where travel was forbidden during a Star Year – was now certain.

An administrative edict had summoned Karolyn's father to join a foraging expedition in the south. At two and a half cycles-old, or fifteen years by the antiquated reckoning, Karolyn had had to grow up fast, now the sole guardian of her brother and sister.

Karolyn's twelve-year-old brother, Michael, paced outside the cottage, arms fidgeting. His fiery red hair underscored his combustible nature. "Let's check the *Wodenwald*. Gretchen will die out there if we do nothing," he choked.

"But Michael, we can't blindly rush into the forest. No one's ever returned from there during a Star Year. We should seek the wise woman's counsel. She'll know what to do."

The children journeyed under a dull gray sky from their cottage on the colony's outskirts toward Crash Hill. Some said the site was cursed. Others believed their ancestors had fallen from the heavens and landed there hundreds of years ago. Karolyn dismissed it as mere fairy tale, an attempt to impose meaning on life's random hardships.

The pair passed scores of colonist-farmers who were struggling to recover from the crippling winter famine that had claimed a third of the population. Cornfields stretched for leagues, interspersed among *woolenshep* grazing land. The six-legged, hoary-haired ruminants paid the children no mind as they chewed on scarlet grasses.

The colony would have plenty of wool for next winter, but the cornhusks' sickly-brown hue presaged a difficult harvest. Thorny violet fireweed inundated the fields, strangling the corn stalks and leaching vital nutrients from the soil. Grim farmers marched in ordered rows, slashing at the infestation with dull machetes. Indigo, burgundy, and golden flora flourished here at the expense of the weaker green. No one knew why. It was just the way of things.

The children followed the decrepit cobblestone road through the vale, and to the ruins near Crash Hill. They found a scarred manor house, with broken white columns lining its ancient portico. Beyond the structure towered

Crash Hill, a ridge rent in two, its exposed granite scraping the gloomy sky. Nary a blade of grass sprouted from its accursed soil.

"We should have gone to the colony center. Olivia won't be happy we're here," Michael warned.

Karolyn also had her doubts, but she kept them to herself. "Don't you want to find your little sister?"

Michael shrugged, and then nodded agreement.

An ornately wrought bird of prey with a brass knocker extending from its claws dominated the center of the manor house's door. Karolyn slinked toward the entrance, hesitated, then rapped the knocker three times.

Silence.

She knocked again with more force.

Something rustled behind the door.

She knocked a third time. A voice rasped, "Go away!"

"Please, hear us out. It's a matter of life and death," Karolyn pleaded.

"Have you lost a child in the *Wodenwald?*"

Karolyn was relieved the wise woman cut to the point. "Yes, my little sister."

"Then there's nothing I can do. That child is lost."

"Surely, something can be done. I won't give up on her."

"Then you're a fool. Go away!"

"Please."

"Leave! Or you'll regret it."

Michael turned to walk away. Karolyn gripped her brother's shoulder.

"We're not leaving until you speak with us," Karolyn demanded.

"Excuse me?" Olivia huffed.

"I said, 'we're not leaving until you speak with us.' No matter what the consequences are."

The woman cackled with amusement. "My, my, aren't we plucky. Fearless little critters aren't we?"

"We are!" Michael chimed in a sudden burst of courage.

Karolyn shook her head. "We take your threats very seriously, ma'am, but we fear losing our sister more."

"Ah, then there may be wisdom in you after all. Enter."

The door swung open revealing a dark threshold. A draft smelling of mint and cinnamon wafted by the children.

The children slipped through the doorway and into a receiving room. Portraits of distinguished women lined the walls. The images fascinated Karolyn. Michael shuffled impatiently.

"Those are portraits of every wise woman since our colony's founding. I am the current caretaker of that long and majestic line." The crone startled Karolyn, but Michael didn't seem surprised. Karolyn guessed it was what had made him anxious all along.

A brown cloak enshrouded Olivia's discolored, wrinkled, and skeletal features. Some say Crash Hill's poisoned soil was responsible for her rotting face. She waved her arm toward a chamber deeper in the manor house. "Follow me."

Olivia led them into a small study lined with ancient tomes and scrolls. She ambled toward a worn wooden desk and sat down. Opposite the desk was a fireplace, where a flickering flame fought to fill the study with some semblance of warmth. An odd staff, consisting of two parallel steel rods that extended outward toward an inverted wooden wedge at its base, lay over the mantle. It was the weirdest object Karolyn had ever seen. Olivia motioned for the children to sit on two creaky chairs facing her desk.

She pulled out a weathered vellum scroll with words scrawled in archaic calligraphic script.

"Vague warnings of an unknown danger in the *Wodenwald* keep most folk away. Yet the most curious among us seek a more nuanced understanding of the world." Olivia faced Karolyn. "You, child, are one of those creatures."

"Please," Karolyn interrupted. "We're losing time. How can we save my sister?"

Olivia's penetrating glare ended all protest. "Patience, child. Without knowledge, time offers no salvation. Patience."

Karolyn nodded.

Olivia continued, "Since our ancestors arrived on this world, they've catalogued the life cycle of the witchwood. Her darkness feeds on mothers' tears, sprouting from the fertile earth every seventy-three years. Some warn that her demon eyes tempt men, or that her scent bewitches them. Others claim that her soothing lullabies put people in a trance that results in death."

The children glanced at each other. Karolyn was uncertain how to respond. Michael spoke first. "There's a witch in the *Wodenwald*?"

Karolyn suppressed a giggle.

Olivia slammed her hand on the table. "Don't dismiss your brother's words, for there is truth in them. Not the entire truth, but enough of it to keep him safe. There's something malevolent haunting the forest, though she's not human. She's something else entirely: a monstrous crossbreed of humanity and the forest driven by a desperate desire to scatter her seed.

"People forget this evil since most colonists experience only one, sometimes two Star Years in their lifetimes. During these years, children vanished never to return. When parents wandered into the forest to find them, they too went missing. You both would do well to heed these warnings, for they reflect centuries of accumulated wisdom."

Karolyn shifted impatiently. She was hearing the same old wives' tales. "I can't accept that. There must be something we can do. According to the lore, no one agrees on which sense the witchwood beguiles. Is it sight, sound, or smell?"

"My, you're an observant child. Is it sight, sound, or smell, indeed? That question has baffled the wisest of us for hundreds of years. But how could one ever answer it? Only a blind and deaf person lacking a nose could do so. And what if they could? What would they do? You can't strike something you can't see, hear, or smell.

"Cut your losses, child. Nothing can be done for your sister now."

The children sat in silence as the dark truth of Olivia's words washed over them.

Then Karolyn said, "Perhaps there is little we can do ourselves, but if we report Gretchen's disappearance to the colony administrator, he may send a search party."

Olivia reddened as she pounded her fist on the table. "You will do no such thing! Losing two more children to the darkness is terrible enough, but losing men who protect and feed the colony is far worse, especially after last winter's famine claimed the lives of so many, including your mother."

Olivia's mention of Tara wounded Karolyn. It took all the willpower the child could muster to avoid bursting into tears. "What if there's a way I can protect the men from the witchwood's enchantments like blocking their ears with cork?"

Olivia furrowed her brow. "Don't speak such nonsense, child. If a two-and-a-half-cycle babe can envision the solution, surely someone's tried before and failed. No. Avoid the *Wodenwald*. Forget your sister."

&

Despondent, Karolyn and Michael trudged through the center of the colony and back toward their cottage. Karolyn had tried her best to put up a good front, to be an example to her younger brother. Now, she could no longer contain her tears.

"What's wrong, child?" a male voice as coarse as gravel asked.

Karolyn raised her head to see the colony administrator's frowning face. A tall, bald man with a flowing white beard, the administrator seemed to carry himself with the arrogance of a small-town politician, confusing popularity for intelligence.

"My sister is lost in the *Wodenwald*."

The administrator raised an eyebrow. "So, go find her."

"I can't. It's a Star Year."

The administrator chortled. His sudden mirth shocked Karolyn.

"The *Wodenwald's* nothing but a forest with few, if any, predators. I'll summon the local militia and have 'em scour it. No reason to worry. We won't let some silly superstition keep us from finding your sister."

Karolyn was hopeful, yet she felt guilty about asking the colony to risk lives on her sister's behalf. She felt obligated to tell the administrator the entire truth.

"Please, sir, don't send them into the forest. Olivia warned me they would be lost. I don't want their blood on my hands. One life is enough."

"Child, you will rue this day for the rest of your life if I don't send men to find your sister."

"Please, if you do send men out, have them take precautions. I have a list of provisions they should carry with them."

The administrator waved his hand in dismissal. "Now, now, child, don't put stock in tall tales conjured up by some batty 'ole coot. Wait at home. The colony will return your sister by the morrow."

∽

Karolyn ignored the administrator's order to stay home. Instead, she gathered the tools members of the search party would need to face the witchwood: cork, beeswax, and bed sheets. Karolyn and her brother loaded them into two sturdy knapsacks before taking them to the men.

True to his word, the administrator had acted quickly. Within two turns of an hourglass, the same time it took the children to locate their supplies, twelve militiamen stood at attention before the colony granary. They were an ad-hoc group of farmers and craftsmen who gathered in times of crisis. Some were well beyond their prime; others, too young. The administrator's edict had called away most of the colony's spare able-bodied men.

The assembled men seemed uneasy about entering the *Wodenwald*.

Karolyn was ecstatic she had caught them before they ventured into the forest. She offered her wares, despite her fear that the administrator would chide her for failing to follow his guidance. Fortunately, the man seemed to let it go. Karolyn wondered if his acquiescence stemmed from a desire to use the children for his own political gain.

"These are Gretchen's siblings," he said as the children approached. "You serve them. Be proud."

Karolyn wasted no time. "Please, take these supplies. The witchwood lying in the forest beyond mesmerizes men with song, light, or scent. Use this cork to plug your ears, the beeswax to fill your nostrils, and a sheet to protect your eyes from her enchantments."

There was an uncomfortable silence. Then the administrator laughed. "Child, how do you expect these men find your sister if they can't see? How can I issue orders if my men can't hear? Go home. Your sister's life is in good hands."

The men hesitated then joined in the administrator's chuckling. Old superstitions died hard, and the men's tentative laughter showed that some were finding it difficult to let them go. Nevertheless, the administrator's appeal to reason won out and the men ignored Karolyn's offer.

"Make sure you pack torches," the administrator said in what Karolyn sensed was an attempt to change the subject. "Since the *Wodenwald* extends several leagues in all directions, we might find ourselves there after nightfall.

Though I doubt torches will be necessary, for the little girl's been missing for only four turns. She couldn't have travelled more than sixteen leagues from the forest's edge.

"I will meet you at the forest in a half turn."

The men saluted, then marched off.

"What now?" Michael asked.

"We're gonna follow them, but we're not going in unprepared. Here." Karolyn handed her brother a gob of beeswax. "Put this in your nostrils." She gave him a blindfold. "And cover your eyes with this."

"But how will I see?"

"Hold my hand. I'll lead you. If I let go for any reason, take hold of me and cover my eyes. If you let go, I'll put cork in your ears. One of us needs to be able to see, and the other needs to hear. We don't know how the witchwood enchants people, so we have to take all precautions. Once we figure out how she does it, we can find a way to save Gretchen."

℞

The children crept through the afternoon shadows as they tracked the patrol through the *Wodenwald*. Thickets of dense yellow shrubs made for slow going. Purple vines twisted and choked the thorny hardwoods rising into a riot of crimson, indigo, and mustard-colored leaves.

"Halt!" A militiaman at the column's vanguard motioned for others to examine his discovery: broken twigs and a child's footprints. As the afternoon wore on, the tracks of Gretchen's passing extended deeper into the forbidden forest.

The afternoon faded into twilight, and twilight blurred into darkness. The men stopped to eat, adjust their bearings, and light their torches. Karolyn and Michael remained hidden among the foliage.

The duo rested too, sharing a husk of corn Karolyn had snagged on her way home from Olivia's manor. Just as Karolyn got comfortable, the men were back on their feet, searching for Gretchen.

Near midnight, the torchlight revealed a garden amidst a wide clearing. At the garden's heart was an array of majestic violet and rose-colored flowers half the size of a man. The flowers were positioned in a hexagonal pattern resembling a six-pointed star. The rose-colored flowers marked the star's edges, while the violet ones clustered around the flowerbed's interior. At the flowerbed's center was the tallest of the violet flowers. Imprinted just under the flower's petals was a disembodied woman's face, one that was vaguely yet uneasily familiar to Karolyn.

A militiaman ambled over to the administrator, whispering in his ear and pointing his torch toward the flowerbed. The cork in Karolyn's ears prevented her from hearing the conversation, though she could deduce the man feared raising his voice might wake the abomination.

Before the administrator answered, the witchwood's beet-red eyes opened and surveyed the men around her. She regarded them with a deep and sinister intelligence, then opened her human mouth and wailed.

Suddenly, it dawned on Karolyn why that face was so familiar. *Mother.*

Karolyn heard nothing, but could see the men stumbling forward as if entranced by the creature's siren song.

Even Michael was not immune. He tore off his blindfold in a fit of mad desperation as the melody lured him toward the flowerbed.

Karolyn wrapped her arms around her younger brother, but he resisted with mindless ferocity. He seemed to possess an uncommon strength somehow amplified by the witchwood's captivating lullaby. Or was it her mother's?

She pulled two corks from her pocket, and stuffed them into Michael's ears while he fought like a wild bull.

Her task completed, it was as if she had lifted her brother from a spell. He was dazed, but no longer in a trance.

The men shambled forward, their heads bobbing in synchronicity to sounds that Karolyn and Michael could not hear, but could feel as the intensity of the dark symphony increased and reverberated throughout the forest.

As men drew closer to the flowers, chords of living vine curled around their throats, hoisting them in the air and tossing them into the barbed maws of mammoth blooms, jaws snapping shut. Karolyn watched in horror as the witchwood devoured the administrator. After securing their prey, the vines tamped out the fallen torches.

Karolyn knew what she had to do.

She gave Michael more cork, touched her ears, and then gestured at the men. Then she was off, racing toward the flowerbed's periphery. If Michael had been strong, the men would be stronger. She jumped on one militiaman's back and held on for dear life as the man flailed. She anchored one arm around his head to maintain balance, while she used her other arm to stuff his ear with cork.

Everything happened so fast. Karolyn saw Michael attempt the same tactic, but the men were too tall. He was also dangerously close to the vines.

After saving one man, Karolyn rushed to grab Michael before the vines did. She pointed to two fallen torches. Then, Karolyn saw something that rattled her to the core. The violet flowers closest to the garden's heart were open, and had young children nestled in their embrace. The children showed varying degrees of violet discoloration. All seemed asleep, oblivious to their sordid condition. She didn't recognize them. Had they been trapped for decades, even centuries? Then she saw Gretchen lying in a pod near the center.

Karolyn wasn't sure if her little sister was alive or dead, but the thought paralyzed her.

Michael acted. He seized a machete from the ground. He sprinted toward a fallen torch, swinging his machete as the vines snapped at him. He severed one, then another, until no vines could reach him. He discarded the blade, picked up the torch, and chucked it into the flowerbed near its edge, letting it burn.

Her brother's example shook Karolyn from her stupor. Seizing a machete, she made her way toward the other torch. The vines swirling around her no longer reached for her legs, but instead aimed for her face.

The militiaman Karolyn had saved was back on his feet, slashing at vines on the clearing's opposite end. The vines shadowing him kept their distance, focusing on his face. Buds on the vines' tendrils sprung open and sprayed him with a black fluid. He dropped to the ground, clawing at his face. The vines fed him to the flowers.

Another vine misted Karolyn with the vile-smelling toxin. She felt lethargic and groggy, but managed to back away from the flowerbed before collapsing. Michael pulled her away from the garden, tears streaming from his eyes.

Michael dragged his sister to a copse of trees. He opened his waterskin and washed the poison from her eyes, nose and throat. Karolyn felt weak, but her brother's quick action had saved her.

The fire on the flowerbed's outskirts was dying. Karolyn wept. It was too much. Her mother. Her sister. So close, yet no way to save them.

A shockwave heralded a chaotic mix of fire and smoke. A vine exploded in a torrent of black ooze. Olivia, cork protruding from her ears, emerged from the clearing carrying the metallic staff Karolyn had noticed at the manor house.

Karolyn could see the witchwood's vines thrashing and twisting in apparent anguish.

Olivia aimed the staff and fired again. Karolyn watched another vine burst. Olivia split the staff in two, inserted two short metal cylinders into the hollow tubes, straightened the staff, and aimed it at another vine. The staff recoiled. Olivia repeated the action, systematically destroying the vines protecting the witchwood.

Olivia turned toward Karolyn and Michael, and signaled them toward the sleeping children.

Karolyn and Michael relit two torches with the waning fire, and plunged into the flowerbed's heart. There, they found their sister among seven other young children in a dream state.

Karolyn didn't think her brother recognized their mother's face. She wanted to keep it that way, so she distracted him with other tasks. She threw a torch at a rose-colored flower and then gestured for Michael to do the same.

Michael sprang into action, while Karolyn carried each child, one by one, away from the flowerbed.

Gretchen was the last child Karolyn saved. As she wrapped her little sister in her arms, she cried with joy though her tears were bittersweet. Burning her mother was no better than burying her.

&

"Never in this colony's history has one so cleverly challenged witchwood. The creature has always emerged from its dark slumber every seventy-three years to spawn and feed. Women far more experienced had attempted to destroy it, but failed. Were it not for the love and dedication of this child, the witchwood would have haunted our descendants. For Karolyn's uncommon bravery and ingenuity, I honor her with the title of novice and pledge to train her in the ways of my craft.

"Karolyn, if your parents were here, they'd be proud."

A tear trickled down Karolyn's cheek.

"I am here!" a male voice shouted from the crowd.

"Father!" Karolyn cried. "I thought you were in the south?"

"I was, but the administrator sent a courier to notify me of Gretchen's disappearance. My commander granted me leave to search for Gretchen. Seems you and Michael already took care of finding her."

Karolyn hugged her brother, father, and sister in a tearful embrace. Olivia turned to Jonas. "May I have a private word with your eldest daughter?"

"For you, anything," Jonas said, smiling.

Karolyn and Olivia walked out of earshot of her family. Karolyn was blunt. "The witchwood will return, won't it?"

Olivia nodded gravely. "The wise women believed the witchwood needed to capture our young to spawn. In a way, it does. Now we've learned it also can sow its seeds on the wind. Your mother's infection proved that. The next time, the colony should burn the body."

"Will you teach me to wield the staff?"

Olivia cackled. "At some point, dear. First, you must learn the story of our origins on this world. Stella, one of the children you saved, will help. The witchwood ensnared her shortly after our ancestors fell from the sky."

END

Afterword

"The Witchwood Whispers" was first published in *Mad Scientist Journal*. The story originated from my desire to write a story that involved the Purple Earth hypothesis, a scientific theory that early Earth favored retinal rather than chlorophyll-based organisms because the sun transmits most of its energy in the green part of the visible spectrum. Organisms photosynthesizing green light would thus absorb green light and reflect other shades like purple, red, orange, or yellow.

The final result turned out to be a science fiction fairy tale against the subtle backdrop of a world populated with flora evolved to photosynthesize green light. The story also includes a not-so-subtle nod to Anton Chekhov's maxim that if a rifle is hanging on the wall in the first act, it must fire in the last act.

What I like most about this story is the world building – imagining a world where the plant life thrives on a different wavelength of visible light than our own. For me, one of the greatest pleasures of writing speculative fiction is dreaming up new, complex, and interesting worlds. I look forward to creating many more.

Movement to First Contact

T he ten-thousand foot crystalline dome towering over what used to be San Francisco reminded Lieutenant McNulty of the man-sized anthills he had seen in the Pacific Northwest. McNulty shuddered at the memory of the anthills' thumb-sized, red-headed, black-bodied architects that had swarmed atop their frightening creations. The main difference between the anthills and this structure was that the dome's outer surface was quiet and lifeless. It was what lurked inside that unnerved him.

"Reaper Six, Reaper One. REDCON One," McNulty transmitted the standard code words over the company radio net to report his platoon's readiness. His tank platoon waited in column on Highway 101, on the city's outskirts as Apache attack helicopters buzzed in the distance, completing another circuit around the structure. The dome's edge extended a few meters beyond what used to be Candlestick Park.

"Reaper One. Reaper Six. Standby for engineers," Captain Dorfman, Lieutenant McNulty's commander, replied.

McNulty's crew shifted in their bulky MOPP suits. Even at a pleasant seventy degrees Fahrenheit, the chemical suits were uncomfortable, and they made fighting and communicating difficult.

"Sir, I got to take a piss," Private Hanson, the tank's loader, broadcasted over the internal communication system.

McNulty rolled his eyes. "Dammit, Hanson! You knew we were going to launch at oh-six hundred, why didn't you take care of it before?"

McNulty already knew the answer. Hanson was a good kid, but a damaged one with suicidal impulses. Once he had turned up with a broken hand due to an "accident." Weeks later, McNulty's men confided to him that Hanson's "accident" had happened after he had punched a seventy-ton Abrams tank over some trifle.

"Never mind," McNulty said. "You're just gonna have to hold it. It's too late to dismount now."

The net was silent for a few moments, then Hanson responded, "Roger, sir."

The engineers were deep inside the tunnel, attaching the final several hundred pounds of C4 to the breach site. They'd been at it for several weeks now. They'd bored a hole small enough for Packbots to get through, but now had to expand the tunnel so tanks could enter the strange structure. The amber-colored translucent substance they were blasting through was stronger than reinforced concrete. After connecting the explosives to a detonation cord, they emerged from the tunnel in preparation for the final explosion.

The crew waited. Sergeant Turner, the tank's gunner, checked and rechecked the tank's weapons systems four or five times. Hanson rocked back and forth. Private First Class Garcia, the nineteen-year old tank driver from Kennett Square, Pennsylvania, hummed hair metal ballads over the tank's intercom from his isolated driver's hole.

"All right gents, as soon as the engineers blast a hole through the dome wall, remember our orders. Under no circumstances are we to open our hatches. The S2 warned us that some of the gasses trapped in this structure react explosively with normal air. Something to do with nitrogen."

McNulty recalled the briefing his platoon had received from Captain Wade, the battalion's intelligence officer, with contempt. The S2 had struggled to explain the technical aspects of the chemical environment the platoon was about to enter. A history major, Wade was clearly out of his depth.

"Yeah, sir," Garcia said, "I remember. It's that silicone stuff chicks put in their tits."

The crew erupted in laughter.

"Garcia, it's silane, not silicone," McNulty reminded him.

The levity was short-lived as the crew prepared for the imminent mission.

"Reaper One. Reaper Six. Fire in the hole. Fire in the hole. Fire in the hole," Dorfman transmitted.

Moments later, the engineers detonated their explosives. A massive cloud of dust and debris resulted, reducing visibility to zero. A steady crescendo of humming resonated from within the structure and near the point of the breach.

"Reaper One. This is Reaper Six. Report."

"Reaper Six. Reaper One. Negative contact. Break. Loud humming is coming from the hole. Permission to cross the LD?" McNulty reported, ending his transmission with a request to cross the line of departure.

"Reaper One, this is Six. Standby."

The crew waited for Captain Dorfman to relay the request up the chain of command. The wait seemed like an eternity to McNulty, and he could sense his crew was growing impatient.

"Sir, what the hell is taking higher so damn long?" Hanson whined.

"This is the first time the military's sending armor into the dome. It's also the Army's first movement to contact mission in an alien environment. The last few Packbots the engineers sent in never returned, and you sure as hell can't send crunchies through," McNulty answered. The term "crunchie" referred to the sound an infantryman's bones made when a tank rolled over one. "The gasses will eat through their MOPP gear and kill 'em. That's why we're going in with tanks. That's also why we cannot, under any circumstances, open our hatches."

"Christ," Hanson cursed, "You mean we won't have any infantry support?"

"That's right. We won't have any artillery support either owing to several tons of rock that will be covering us throughout our mission," McNulty said, shrugging.

Moments later, the order finally came down, "Reaper One. Reaper Six. Permission granted. Go. Go. Go."

McNulty issued the command to his tank platoon, and led the column of four seventy-ton Abrams tanks into the smoldering hole left by the engineers.

The armor rolled through the breach. The tanks' turbine engines whirled against the overpowering hum echoing throughout the crystal lattice structure. The tanks passed through a hundred-meter thick wall of crystalline silica, before they reached the other side, and into the dome's inner cavity.

"Start scanning," McNulty ordered over his platoon's intercom system, "Report any movement. Remember the rules of engagement. Don't shoot anything until you get my order. There could still be civilians out there."

McNulty doubted his last point. Nothing could possibly survive in this toxic environment.

The platoon headed along its planned axis of advance from Highway 101 to Highway 280, where it halted at its first checkpoint.

"Reaper Six. Reaper One. Radio check, over," McNulty reported to headquarters as planned. He was disheartened by the lack of a response, though he had anticipated it. McNulty attempted a similar radio check with his platoon. To his chagrin, there was no response.

"Radio still ain't working, sir," Garcia said. McNulty could always count on Garcia to state the obvious.

"The radio's working fine, but for some reason radio waves don't propagate inside the dome. The S2 said the NASA boys at Moffett Field think the EM spectrum's been saturated inside this structure. It's not really surprising we can't communicate with headquarters or the rest of the platoon. We'll just have to make do with the communications techniques we practiced in training," McNulty said over the tank's intercom. "We knew going in that radio comms might not work, especially after the first Packbots didn't return."

McNulty had drilled his platoon on alternatives to radio communications. Nevertheless, the platoon's inability to communicate using its radios would be yet another impediment, like the MOPP suits, to McNulty's ability to maneuver and control his platoon.

"Garcia, tap your brake lights twice. It's time to move out," McNulty ordered.

The armored column roared back to life and advanced up Highway 280, along the southeastern outskirts of the city and toward its next objective.

As the platoon edged closer toward San Francisco's financial district, the humming became louder and increased in frequency. The steady resonance sounded like the otherworldly chirps of metallic cicadas. McNulty sensed his crew's uneasiness. It was not the eerie lack of human activity in the cityscape ahead that bothered McNulty so much as the lack of human remains. How could hundreds of thousands of people disappear without leaving behind any sign of their passing?

"Sir, don't you think it's kinda odd there aren't any cars on the freeway?" Sergeant Turner offered, "I mean, you'd think when the meteorite's fragments solidified around the city, and the silane gas suffocated the drivers, there would still be cars and car wrecks leading all the way to the heart of the city. What gives?"

McNulty had observed the same thing; he just didn't think it would help morale to say it out loud.

"I'd noticed. Maybe some folks did survive," McNulty answered in a half-hearted effort to put a positive spin on the mystery.

"No way, sir. Something took 'em! You said yourself that nothing can survive here!" Hanson panicked.

"Calm down, Hanson. Everything is going according to plan. We're about halfway to our objective at the Transamerica Pyramid. Once we get there, we'll link up with second platoon, which is advancing from the Bay Bridge. We'll then proceed together toward the Bay Bridge, and back to friendly territory."

"Sir, I've got AT&T Park on my right," Turner said.

"Driver, turn left on Third Street and reduce your speed to 20 klics. Turner, keep scanning. We're about to enter a built up area, so I want everyone alert."

"All right, gents," McNulty addressed his crew, "We're about to hit our third checkpoint at Market Street. Use this as an opportunity to check your equipment and…"

THUD! THUD! THUD!

The crew's tank shook from some unknown impact.

"What the hell was that?" McNulty said as he tried to make sense of what had slammed into the tank. "Turner, continue scanning!"

TUNK, TUNK, TUNK. TUNK, TUNK, TUNK.

"Gunner, follow those fifty cal tracers," McNulty ordered. "It looks like Sergeant Johnson's tank is engaging something."

"Sweet Jesus!" Turner yelled, "Do you see that, sir?"

McNulty looked into his sight. "Holy crap, put your thermals on!"

McNulty's screen lit up with seven or eight contacts, each the size of a horse. They were bounding toward the column, and launching projectiles from what appeared to be scorpion-like tails.

McNulty's training took over.

"Contact! Enemy. Front." McNulty transmitted over the platoon net from habit. Realizing the other tanks wouldn't receive his transmission, he then switched to the internal net and said, "Garcia, hit the brakes three times. We need to get the platoon on line."

The platoon wheeled into position, orienting its tanks toward the advancing contacts in a single horizontal line to maximize its collective firepower.

"Son of a bitch! The fifty cal didn't even make that thing flinch," Turner said. "Looks like we should try something a little stronger. Whaddaya say, sir?"

McNulty nodded.

"Gunner – HEAT – seven hostiles – nearest hostile!" McNulty commanded. The crew leaped into action.

"Identified!" Turner declared, alerting McNulty he had the M1A2's one hundred twenty-millimeter smoothbore cannon trained on the first target. The ammo door at the turret's rear compartment opened, and Hanson grabbed a HEAT round from the ready rack, a honeycombed chamber teaming with rounds. HEAT was an acronym for High Explosive Anti-Tank that tankers used to destroy lightly armored targets. He shoved it into the main gun's breech, jumped out of the cannon's path of recoil, and reported, "Up!" to notify McNulty that he was out of the way.

"Fire!"

"On the waaay," Turner reported as he pulled the trigger and a HEAT round sped toward its target at over a thousand meters per second. A familiar clang sounded as the HEAT round's cylindrical brass AFCAP hit the turret floor.

The round hit the thing closest to the tank dead center and propelled it about twenty meters into an adjacent building in a riot of dust and debris.

"Target!" McNulty announced.

McNulty listened as the rest of his platoon blasted away at the strange entities. His men used a carefully rehearsed escalation of weaponry per the platoon's rules of engagement. First, they'd use machine guns. If the machine guns failed, they'd use HEAT rounds. If HEAT rounds failed, they'd fire SABOT rounds – high energy, kinetic rounds designed to penetrate heavily armored targets.

To McNulty's dismay, the first target got back on its six black spindly legs and charged at the platoon.

"Gunner – SABOT – hostile. Near hostile!"

"Identified!"

"Up!"

"Fire!"

"On the waaay!"

The SABOT round struck home. The high velocity, depleted uranium round created enough overpressure that it sucked the creature's insides out of it as the round passed through the target at over fifteen hundred meters per second. Soon the rest of the platoon was firing SABOT rounds, making quick work of the encroaching enemy.

In the heat of battle, McNulty had blocked out the strange metallic droning in the background. Now he couldn't ignore it. Almost as if in response to the engagement, the pitch became higher and the sound's intensity increased.

"Driver, flash your front headlights once," McNulty ordered Garcia to signal to his platoon that his tank was still fully mission capable.

When the other three tanks responded in kind, McNulty breathed a sigh of relief. "Alright, let's move out. Garcia, give 'em the signal."

"WHAT THE HELL! WE'RE GONNA DIE!" Hanson screamed. He cradled his head with his arms and rocked back and forth. "You're all insane! They're everywhere! We gotta turn back. Now!"

"Get your shit together!" McNulty raised his voice. "We have a mission to complete, and our country is depending on us. We aren't going to turn back until we determine what's emitting that EM signal from the vicinity of the

Transamerica Pyramid. The people at NASA think it's the one place in this whole godforsaken complex where these bugs are communicating with something in space."

"No way, sir. I'm not doing it. No way."

"If you don't, you'll be court-martialed when we get back."

"We ain't gettin' back, sir."

"Sergeant Turner. Remove Hanson's service weapon," McNulty ordered.

Turner sprung to his feet and thrust his elbow under Hanson's gas mask, pinning him up against the tank's ammo door. "Surrender your nine millimeter, or I'm going to rip off your mask, and you WILL die," Turner threatened.

Hanson seemed stunned and did nothing as Turner removed the sidearm.

In any normal tactical environment, McNulty would force Hanson out of the tank and send him to the rear. Turner would then act as loader, and transfer control of the weapons systems to McNulty's commander's station. However, forcing Hanson out of the vehicle would guarantee his death and doom the rest of the crew, as toxic silane gas would build up inside the tank's hull. McNulty felt he was left with only one suboptimal solution.

"Hanson," McNulty addressed the soldier in a reassuring tone. "I know you've just been through a crazy event, but you survived. Whatever's out there, we can kill it. If you just keep your cool, and we all work together, we can get out of this alive. You have two options: Stay in the tank and fight, or get out and die. What'll it be?"

Hanson returned to his post, slouching back onto his seat.

The platoon split into two-tank sections with one section moving forward, while the other covered the advance from an overwatch position.

"Garcia. Stop the tank," McNulty commanded. "Does anyone hear that?"

"Hear what, sir? I can't hear anything anymore," Turner answered.

"That's what worries me. The humming's stopped."

"Why do you think it's stopped, sir?" Turner asked.

"I don't know. Let's keep moving. Garcia, give the signal for the other tanks to move out."

The column crept along Kearny Street. The tanks' turrets rotated back and forth, scanning the buildings towering above them.

The absence of automobiles and bodies continued to weigh on McNulty. *Where the hell did everyone go?* he wondered.

"Garcia, we're only a few blocks away from the objective. We need to turn right here on California Street."

The city remained deathly quiet as the platoon turned and made its push toward its intermediate objective on Montgomery Street.

McNulty moved his head back from the commander's sights to check on Hanson. The boy still didn't seem right in the head. Turner continued to view the outside environment through the limited lens of his gunner's sight.

"Oh my God! Sir, I think I know where all the cars and people went," Turner shuddered, "They..."

A high-frequency whine cut off the sergeant. McNulty pressed the lenses of his gas mask back against the commander's sight.

"Hostiles! Twelve o'clock!" Turner shouted as he observed a large number of black silhouettes descending toward the tanks from the surrounding high-rises.

This time, the creatures weren't firing spikes at the tanks, but advancing toward them.

"Gunner – SABOT – Hostiles. Near hostile!"

"Identified!"

"Up!"

"On the waaay!"

The tank shook in recoil and one of the assailants burst into shards of rock and sand. Chunks of rock and debris rained down on the tank as the SABOT round passed through its target and into a hotel across the street. McNulty's wingman, Sergeant Rogers, blasted another hostile from his tank. Rogers' main gun engaged targets from left to right while McNulty worked from the opposite direction.

The two tanks ahead of Sergeant Rogers's and McNulty's had also stopped to join the fight.

As the platoon fired SABOT after SABOT, the creatures kept coming.

"Loader, ammo check!" McNulty commanded.

"Ten SABOT rounds remaining, sir," Hanson responded, then added, "I told you we were gonna die."

"Fuck. Fuck. Fuck," McNulty swore. "Calm down, Hanson."

McNulty considered for a moment. "Alright, here's what we're gonna do. If second platoon had gotten this far, we'd have heard them fighting these things by now. We need to get to the Bay Bridge ASAP. The most important thing we can do is pass on what we've learned about these creatures to headquarters."

"Sounds like a plan, sir," Turner said.

"Garcia, drive close enough to the front of Sergeant Johnson's tank so we can signal him that we're turning around. Do it fast."

Garcia complied by throttling the tank to its maximum speed. Before he could reach Sergeant Johnson's tank, the crew watched a horde of aliens flood from the buildings around them. They reached Sergeant Johnson's tank and were laboring to overturn it.

"Driver, stop!" McNulty yelled. He then issued more fire commands.

"Sir, we might hit Sergeant Johnson's tank," Sergeant Turner warned.

"If we don't do anything, he's dead anyway."

The SABOT ripped along the street, rendering its target into a burning hulk. The target was so close that its stony remains hit McNulty's tank.

"What the hell was that?" Garcia asked.

"Alien gut," McNulty said.

"What the heck are these things made out of, sir?" Turner asked.

"The Moffett nerds think it's silicon."

"You mean, like in sand and rocks and stuff?"

"Something like that."

The three other tanks fought to eliminate the swarms overrunning Sergeant Johnson's tank, but the creatures kept coming.

SABOT rounds whipped through the streets and between the tanks as the creatures swarmed over the platoon. Sergeant Johnson's tank was littered with them. His tank could no longer move forward or backward as the creatures began to push it toward the center of the domed structure.

"Sir, we need to get out of here," Turner warned. "There's no saving Sergeant Johnson's crew."

"I won't leave 'em behind. Keep fighting."

The three operational tanks continued firing SABOTs at their attackers, but soon the enemy was on the verge of overrunning them too.

"Screw this, sir, I'm turning the tank around!" Garcia said.

Before McNulty could countermand Garcia, the tank jolted into reverse, and then executed a sharp U-turn back up California Street and past the two remaining tanks. As they passed the rest of the platoon, dozens of the spindly silicoids overtook the pair of tanks Garcia left behind.

The humming had begun in earnest the instant the second attack began, and was now at a fever pitch as McNulty's crew abandoned twelve of the platoon's men.

Garcia throttled the tank to its top speed as he maneuvered the seventy-ton monster up the hill and back toward Kearny, retracing the platoon's original path into the city. McNulty judged that Garcia had unilaterally abandoned any hope of reaching the Bay Bridge.

"Garcia, slow down!" McNulty ordered just as Garcia made a hard right turn into one the creatures at over forty miles an hour.

The tank bulled right through the thing. From his front right periscope, McNulty saw the creature fall to the side of the tank minus several of its arachnid-like limbs.

As the tank continued forward, it lurched to the right. A dull mechanical whine followed. McNulty worried the silicoid's shorn appendages were entangled with the tank's wheel assembly.

"Sir, we threw track!" Garcia screamed, confirming McNulty's fears.

Of all the things that could go wrong with this mission, the fact that something so mundane would doom them was almost comical to McNulty. He figured that the creature's limbs had gotten tangled in the tank's track, and somehow cut through the rubber treads, rendering forward movement impossible. What a clusterfuck.

"Prepare to defend in place," McNulty said, trying to ignore the fact that one of his subordinates had so overtly disobeyed his orders.

On the outside, the incessant whine continued to reverberate. Inside the tank, there was silence.

"What the hell was that?" Hanson interrupted the strangely comforting deadman's truce as a loud tapping echoed throughout the tank. More tapping started in from all directions. Then the tank began to rock.

"They're all over us!" Garcia shouted over the intercom.

More silence.

"Turner, you said you saw what happened to all the cars and people. Now's the time to speak up," McNulty ordered.

"Sir, those things were using the metal from cars to build some sort of inner wall in this structure. I could see steel all wrapped into what looked like some sort of twisted mechanical web."

The rocking of the tank and the rapping on the outer armor intensified.

"What about the people?"

Turner hesitated and then spoke. "Well, sir. I can't be sure of what I saw. They...I saw...shapes...human shapes...suspended from the buildings. Like cocoons."

"Screw this, sir! I'm getting out of here!" Hanson shrieked.

Turner stretched across the breech to stop Hanson, but Hanson's right cross to Turner's gas mask caught the gunner completely unaware, knocking him unconscious.

McNulty reached for his nine millimeter, but Hanson was on him and thrashing at McNulty's gas mask before the lieutenant could pull the trigger.

Two shots rang out.

∽

Death would have been a better fate. At least McNulty would have remained human. Now he was turning into something else. Enshrouded in hardened silicon crystal lattice, time felt slower and his affinity with humanity faded away.

The creature known as McNulty would be useful to the hive, even with a third of its brain matter dead and gone. The McNulty entity was one of them now, and the hive would soon establish its dominion over this world.

∽

Six hours after the two platoons from Alpha Troop failed to reach their checkpoints on time and as planned, Colonel Brown decided to commit the entire Regiment.

He felt sorry for Captain Dorfman, who had lost two-thirds of his Troop in an operation he hadn't had the opportunity to oversee himself. It was lamentable, but they had their orders.

৯৩

A week later, a mass similar in size to the original meteorite ejected from the San Francisco structure. Based on the object's trajectory, NORAD projected it would land on New York City within the hour.

END

Afterword

"Movement to First Contact" was the first serious speculative short story I wrote. Ironically, it was also my first short fiction sale to *Plasma Frequency Magazine* in 2013. While I wrote this tale in early October 2011, it never felt quite right, so I kept refining and revising it. I didn't submit it anywhere until October of the following year, even though I still thought it was my weakest story at the time. They say an author is the worst judge of his or her work. That this piece was my first short fiction sales lends credence to this claim.

The story's title derives from a play on two different concepts – a movement to contact and first contact. In the military, a movement to contact mission is one in which a military unit maneuvers toward another moving enemy unit. When they collide, a battle ensues. In this case, the movement to contact mission involves first contact with an alien species that had infested a major American city.

The concept for the ten thousand foot crystalline dome was inspired by my experiences with Western thatching ants (*Formica obscuripes*) while training at Fort Lewis, Washington as a young cadet in the summer of 1997. These ants built mounds out of twigs and pine needles that stood as high as two meters. And they were everywhere. I fondly remember conducting night land navigation and hearing cadets scream after stumbling into one of these mounds. The individual ants were so big, you could see their black eyes on bright red heads. The ants would frequently feast on cadets who had the misfortune of laying in an ant horde's path while those cadets established a firing position. These insects both revolted and fascinated me.

As for the rest of the story, I drew on my experiences as a former tank platoon leader and cavalry troop executive officer. I wanted to give readers a real sense of the constraints under which soldiers must operate when they fight in a chemical environment (like buttoned-up turrets and the wearing of MOPP gear). I further handicapped my protagonist by taking away his ability to use radio communications. Ultimately, I wanted to limit my protagonist's freedom of action so I could increase the story's dramatic tension. I hope you're satisfied with the result.

White Nights, Mammon's City

It was late again and Karl Reeve's stims were running low. His heart monitor predicted cardiac arrest within twenty-four hours if he didn't sleep soon.

Karl stared out his building's windows, distracted by memories of his father. Rays of an unsetting sun glinted off vast diamond towers sprinkled with flakes of gold and platinum. He watched frenetic financial wizards representing thousands of diverse species hustle past through a city that freed them from the constraints of darkness.

The sun always shined on Karl's side of Zeta Reticulum B, a tidally locked world over thirty-nine light years from Earth. It was an ideal location for an interplanetary investment bank where dreams of forever finance became reality.

Karl specialized in interplanetary mergers and acquisitions. When an interstellar conglomerate wanted to buy a world, they hired his firm, Screwtape Rearden.

Because of the planetary stakes involved, his work required herculean effort and an unrelenting attention to detail. Yet exhaustion and worry today kept bringing him back to thoughts of his father. When Karl was ten, his dad was larger than life. As the cicadas had chirped lazily in the muggy August air, Karl and his dad had tuned out the world. All movement had slowed to the cadence of the baseball, its stitching twisting through space and time, until the snap of a glove had heralded its arrival. Then the cycle had begun anew marked by the peak and trough of throw and catch, action and reaction, yin and yang.

That man of vigor now lay crippled and shivering in his bed on Earth, riddled with pus-encrusted sores. Karyakin's Syndrome. Karl's father didn't have long. Two, maybe three months. But Karl still had a year left on his contract, and couldn't yet afford the exorbitant cost to travel home.

Karl was a junior analyst, a white-collar slave. He held a position requiring the most work and conferring the least prestige. He conjured up senior bankers' whims into neatly formatted three-dimensional matrices of reality from the close of business to the crack of dawn. That is, if there had been a dawn.

The deal was a big one, a once-in-a-generation transaction that could make or break a senior banker's career. Everything was hush-hush. Not even the senior bankers competing for the business knew the buyer's name or the target world's location. They had to conduct all business through a legal intermediary.

The bonus from this transaction was supposed to have made it all worthwhile. Karl's loans paid off, he would've been free to do whatever the hell he'd wanted wherever he'd wanted. He had planned to use his bonus to buy a one-way ticket off this psychotic rock and back to Earth to see his father one last time. But Karl was a year late and a million credits short.

Karl's boss, Rango Xen, was eager to get started on the pitch. "Karl, we should do a geologically-staged discounted cash flow analysis on all the target planet's mineral resources."

Five hours of work, Karl thought.

Rango was a native Reticulan. His reptilian species didn't sleep – an adaptation honed from millions of years of evolution in an ecosystem where the sun never set. It was also an ideal quality for an interstellar investment banker. Being cold-blooded didn't hurt either.

"We should also construct multiple scenarios valuing the target planet based on a variety of different industrial development paradigms. We should also forecast them out to four billion years," Rango said.

Part of being a successful analyst was asking the right questions to preempt too much work. "Would three scenarios be sufficient?" Karl asked. Three was a ridiculously low number that Rango was likely to reject. But Karl needed to set Rango's expectations low.

Ten hours of continuous work, Karl estimated.

"No. We should do fifteen scenarios. Our client will be more impressed."

Fifty hours of continuous work.

One of the "joys" of interplanetary investment banking was the teamwork. Everybody said things like: "we should do this" and "we should show that", but when it was time to buckle down, the senior banker had already gone home. While Rango didn't do any of the legwork, he never slept, so Karl could always count on the Reticulan to check in on him at all hours.

"I will review a holodraft when I return in twelve hours. Thanks." Rango said and then left Karl's cubicle.

"You're not gonna finish in time, are you?" a female voice sneered from an adjacent cubicle.

Lindsey.

Every time Karl heard her voice a wave of revulsion washed over him. But when he saw her, he couldn't concentrate.

Lindsey sauntered over to Karl's cubicle, smelling of rose shampoo. Her emerald eyes regarded Karl like a bird of prey might consider a rodent. "Looks like you're about to collapse. Want some stims?" She offered Karl two olive-colored horse pills.

"Why are you giving me these?"

"You seem like you could use 'em. Am I wrong?"

Karl hesitated, and then said, "No, you're not wrong. Ah…Thanks."

"Happy to help." Lindsey smiled and returned to her cubicle.

Karl couldn't figure her out. He'd suspected she'd relayed information about his comings and goings to Rango, especially when Karl was late. Maybe she'd sensed he no longer trusted her, and felt guilty. Perhaps she wanted to make amends. He was willing to give her the benefit of the doubt, so he popped the stim, then tried to jam over two Earth days of work into twelve hours. Karl was fully aware there was a chance his stim use could kill him. Yet when he balanced this uncertainty against the risk of losing his job, he decided to roll the dice.

ℂ

Rango's image appeared on Karl's holoberry. "Karl. What happened? You look awful."

Karl lifted his drool-lathered cheek from the desk. He was lucky he remembered who he was. Weeks without sleep sometimes resulted in dissociative amnesia among humans. Karl hadn't had an episode yet, but now was as good a time as any.

"What time is it?" Karl asked.

The tone of Rango's voice dropped an octave. "You don't have a holodraft ready, do you?"

Karl checked the chronometer below Rango's image. Crap. The holodraft was due in ten minutes. Karl looked up at Rango. "No, I don't."

Karl struggled with reading alien emotions, but after spending nearly every waking hour with Rango for the past year, he knew when Rango's jaw tightened and his neck frill tensed, it was bad. Real bad.

"I should never have hired a human. I thought it would help me develop more relationships with interstellar congloms. So far, all it's gotten me is an amnesia-riddled junior analyst who rarely gets his work done on time.

Fortunately, Lindsey took the initiative and did your work for you. She uploaded a holodraft ten minutes ago."

What the hell? Karl thought. Then it dawned on him why the stim didn't work.

Interplanetary investment banking was a competitive business – swimming with the sharks and such. Lindsey was no exception. Yet on a strange world, a pretty face from one's own species went a long way when it came to trust. Stupid. Stupid.

Rango continued. "If this deal didn't require two full-time analysts, I would've terminated your employment after this incident. Don't let it happen again."

"Two analysts?"

"Two *human* analysts," Rango emphasized the word "human". "I need someone continuously available, and your species unfortunately doesn't perform well without sleep."

Karl nodded. "Right, I'll get back to work immediately."

"You'd better. And remember what I said." Rango's hologram winked out.

Then Karl realized that Lindsey unwittingly gave him some needed rest, just not enough of it. His heart monitor was now out of the red and into the yellow.

Lindsey scoffed and said, "I see you've decided to rejoin the living. I trust you enjoyed your nap?"

"No, I didn't. Nor did I appreciate your sabotaging me."

"What're you talking about? I deserve some gratitude for bailing you out of that situation."

"Bailing me out? Is that what you call slipping me a tranq pill?"

Lindsey huffed and said, "Screw you. I gave you a stim. You were probably just too far gone to benefit from it."

"If you were trying to help me, why didn't you just wake me up? Why is your name all over the holodraft?"

That shut her up.

Lindsey infuriated Karl, but retaliation was not an option. In the universe of interplanetary high finance, Karl saw two kinds of junior analysts — those with three-point-nine GPAs from IIT, Stanford, Harvard, and Oxford, and those who were the children of interplanetary conglom leaders, many of whom grew up on paradise planets like Gaia Five. Lindsey was the latter – born on third base, thinking she'd hit a triple.

If the bank terminated Lindsey, it might forgo future transactions worth quadrillions of credits. But Karl was easily replaceable. He had to tread carefully if he'd ever hope to return home. Staying on this world for any longer than another year was dangerous. Most humans committed suicide after two years of exposure to a sun that never set. After spending a year here, Karl was frequently irritable and easily distractible, classic signs of hypomania.

৪৩

A personal call flashed on Karl's holoberry. His heart skipped a beat. Was it his mother? He didn't know what he'd do if his father died today.

The call had to be from Earth. He didn't have friends anywhere else. Karl checked the call's point of origin. The signal was restricted and encrypted.

Now Karl was intrigued.

After Karl accepted the call, the image of a squat muffin-shaped being appeared on his holoberry. A forest of eyestalks protruded from the creature's dorsal surface and articulated limbs extended at equal intervals along its circumference.

"Hello," Karl said.

"Karl Reeves, I presume?"

"Yes."

"Excellent. My name is Glorglin Ugoglin. I represent the human resources department at Mandrake and Wormwood. We're looking to fill an analyst position in our Zeta Reticulum B office. Do you know anyone who might be interested?"

Interesting, Karl thought. *Mandrake and Wormwood was even more prestigious than Screwtape Rearden. This call was definitely worth taking.*

"I may know of someone," Karl said.

"Good, good. If you can have them contact me using this secure channel within forty-eight hours, I would appreciate it. Good day."

The recruiter's image disappeared.

Karl thought seriously about the position. He could start over without the threat of termination hanging over him. Then he shrugged it off. He didn't relish having to prove himself to another group of strangers. No. He would fulfill his obligations to Screwtape Rearden because, for all its warts, the firm had been the only one to take a chance on him when no other firm would.

⋅⋅⋅

"We won the mandate!" Rango's frilled neck undulated. "We're going with the wild card scenario."

"Scenario fifteen?" Karl asked, incredulous.

"That's right. We need to do some more extensive modeling on that scenario. It's going to be a hostile takeover."

Karl shuddered. In the hallowed lore of Terran investment banking, a hostile takeover had put fear into the hearts of a company's management team. To protect their clients against private equity vulture capitalists, investment bankers had devised creative defenses to forestall these barbarians at the gate. This so-called shark repellent had included a host of procedural and structural defenses such as staggered boards, poison pills, and dozens of other devices and gimmicks to help management retain control. In the twenty-third century, the hostile takeover of a planet held far grimmer implications.

"Great!" Karl lied. "What's the target planet?"

"That's highly confidential. Only a select number of people at our firm need to know, and you are not one of them."

"Then how can I do any of the financial modeling?"

"The buyers are sanitizing the data. You will have all the relevant numbers, but all names and locations will be encoded."

"Do we know who the buyer is?" Karl asked.

"A Centauran conglom."

Karl cringed. Centauran-run congloms had a reputation for carelessly upending planetary ecosystems to extract mineral resources. And Centaurans weren't particularly fond of humans.

☙

The preliminary data hit Karl's desk shortly after his firm won the mandate. The target world's atmosphere was just under eighty percent nitrogen and a little over twenty percent oxygen. The planet's liquid water oceans covered slightly over seventy percent of the planet.

Not good.

The client also expressed a particular interest in extracting molten metals from the planet's mantle.

Not good at all.

Karl rationalized that Earth wasn't the only world that had these specific atmospheric and surface characteristics. In a galaxy as large as the Milky Way, there had to be others. Or so he hoped.

The next sixteen hours alternated between his checking his increasingly noisy heart monitor and his running the numbers to determine what the target world was worth.

Karl felt lightheaded and dizzy, and his heart beat at an irregular rhythm. The more Karl ran the numbers, the more one thing became clear: only a single world matched the data.

ॐ

Karl spent the next several days in a work-fueled haze. He felt powerless. Within several months, nearly everyone he'd ever known would be gone. Only those few humans who'd left Earth would survive the genocide.

He would be the executioner's assistant, the ordinary man complicit in an extraordinary crime. And there was nothing he could do about it. His impotence only deepened his sorrow at missing his father's final days.

The only thing Karl thought to do was share his grim discovery with the nearest member of his species.

"Ridiculous," Lindsey scoffed. "No one's done a hostile takeover in over a century, and the first takeover target just happens to be Earth? That's rich, even for you."

Karl was beginning to regret revealing his findings, yet he persisted. "Don't believe me? Take another look at the data. You've been working with it now for as long as I have."

Lindsey rolled her eyes. "I have more important work to do." A three dimensional matrix from a different transaction materialized around her workspace.

"Please, Lindsey. Just check."

She ignored him.

He ran to the break room, poured a cup of water and returned to Lindsey's cubicle, where he tossed water onto her holoterminal.

"What the hell!" Lindsey yelled.

Karl raised his hands defensively. "Don't worry. Everything is still saved on the network, and the firm can replace your terminal. In the meantime, why don't you hang out in my office?"

Lindsey was trembling. Her face was beet red. "Fine!"

When she arrived in Karl's office, Karl had a three-dimensional model of Earth running in geological real-time.

"What's this?" Lindsey said.

"It's my section of the holopresentation. It outlines how our clients can most efficiently extract molten iron from the target's mantle."

"Why'd you make it look like Earth?"

"I didn't. I just entered the data into the matrix, and this is the holoterminal's resulting visualization."

Lindsey's eyes widened. She drew her hand to her mouth. "My God."

Karl grabbed Lindsey by the shoulders. "Lindsey, I know we haven't seen eye to eye since we've been at the firm. But we have to put all that behind us. We can't let this transaction happen."

જી

"Where are the holodocs?" Rango asked.

Talk about a cold start. Karl looked up from his drool-besotted desk in confused exhaustion. "Huh?"

"Huh? That's all you have to say? The management team will be here in fifteen minutes!" Rango's neck frill flared.

Karl popped a stim pill. "Right! I'm on it!"

Karl gestured toward his holographic display sensors and watched a complex array of numbers spring to life. Five billion years of geologic time passed in minutes as his forecasts progressed from the extinction of all indigenous species to the rapacious extraction of the target world's mineral resources.

Rango ceased his frill-flaring the instant he saw Karl's simulation. "It seems you aren't so worthless after all."

Self-conscious, Karl said, "I'll join you in about five minutes. I need to clean myself up for the meeting."

Rango's jaw tightened. "I don't think that's a good idea."

Then it hit Karl. These were Centaurans. They were the first sentient species humanity had encountered when humans started exploring the stars.

The encounter was an unfortunate one since it took humans over half a century to discover that the "animals" they raised, butchered, and ate were a telepathic and sentient species. After that discovery, humanity had tried to make things right with the Centaurans, but the Centaurans refused to forgive or forget.

"I see," Karl said.

Rango nodded, and left for the meeting.

Karl checked his heart monitor: deep red. He put his head on his desk and took a power nap to stay alive.

∾

"You buffoon!" Rango screamed in his trilling Zeta Reticulan voice, "You handed me the wrong scenario! You embarrassed me in there. If not for my quick thinking, we would have lost the mandate."

"Huh?" Karl said, feigning surprise. "But you asked for scenario fifteen. I handed you scenario fifteen."

"No! I asked for scenario fifteen point three. You handed me an earlier draft, which had some noticeable and unforgiveable errors. Fortunately, I used the Centaurans' contempt for humanity to explain away the mistake. Consider this your last warning."

Karl nodded. "Yes, sir. It won't happen again."

Rango stormed out of Karl's office, neck frill flaring.

Lindsey entered shortly thereafter. "He didn't take that very well."

"No, he didn't. But it looks like we bought ourselves another week or so of time. Not too shabby."

"Now what do we do? The transaction's still gonna happen, no?"

"Probably. Next time a simple delay isn't gonna work. We have to convince the Centaurans not to do the transaction."

"I agree, but how do we accomplish that?"

"We convince them that the target world is too expensive," Karl said with a smile.

ะი

"Are you sure you did the right analysis?" Rango asked.   "Absolutely. We ran through every scenario you outlined," Karl said.

Rango's eyes shifted to Lindsey. "Is this true?"

"Yes. Some industry analysts are projecting commodity prices to rise dramatically over the next several billion years. No matter how we analyze the data, the price for Planet X rises by at least twenty-five percent."

"I hate to say this, but I don't think the Centaurans are gonna do this transaction at that price," Karl said.

"Don't tell me what price they're in or out. I'll determine that," Rango said. "There must be a valuation technique that yields a lower price. Did you calculate the planet's liquidation value?"

"Of course," Karl answered. "It was about twenty percent lower than what we think the asset's fair market value will be. No interstellar conglom worth its salt would sell an asset at such a discount."

Rango fumed. "Alright. Let me think. Maybe we can convince the Centaurans to purchase a minority stake in Planet X and acquire additional shares over time. I want you two to run five scenarios tonight on this option and supply me with a holodraft in four hours."

ะი

The image of a Pictorian female empath materialized on Karl's holoberry.

"I'm sorry to disturb you, Mr. Reeves, but I have some bad news."

Here it comes.

"Unfortunately, we are eliminating your position. I am here to discuss our very generous benefits package, which is displayed here for your convenience." She pointed at a holodoc that appeared in the air.

Karl felt nauseated. "I've just lost my job?"

"I'm afraid so, Mr. Reeves. As I noted earlier, we've provided you with a very generous severance, and…"

"Wait," Karl interrupted. "Why am I being fired? What did I do wrong?"

"Not fired, Mr. Reeves, but your position has been eliminated. I'm very sorry to be the bearer of bad news, but if you'll please take a look at our very generous benefits package, you'll see that…"

Karl shut off his holoberry. Rango owed him an explanation. When he turned to exit his office, two brutish Reticulans stood outside his door.

"You have thirty minutes to pack your belongings and exit the building," one said.

Karl stood in silence, uncertain what to do.

Lindsey passed Karl's cubicle, glanced at Karl with an expression that looked like pity, and walked away.

Was she in on this? Did she use me? he thought.

Karl packed his things and left with his dignity barely intact.

⌘

Karl spent the next few hours moping around his apartment. His life was over. His severance was nowhere near what he needed to book transit back to Earth. Hell, it was barely enough to pay for one long-range transmission home.

His holoberry beeped. Lindsey's image appeared. She was in tears.

"Yeah?" Karl said, making no effort to conceal his disgust.

"Karl, I'm so sorry about what happened. It's not right."

"Yeah, whatever. You probably knew it was coming, didn't you? Hell, you probably had something to do with it."

"No-o-o," she cried. "I swear I had nothing to do with it. If I weren't the only analyst left, I'd've been laid off, too." Lindsey then took a deep breath and said, "Karl, Rango knows."

"What?"

"He knows we inflated the price. He had me rerun the numbers using more optimistic projections. The Centaurans are still doing the deal."

"What?" Karl was apoplectic. Not only had he lost his job, but also he faced the prospect of losing nearly everyone he'd ever known.

"Why, Lindsey? Why did you help him?"

"I didn't have a choice," she sobbed. "He'd have fired me too."

"You selfish bitch." Karl regretted the words the instant they left his mouth. Lindsey exploded in a torrent of tears.

"I didn't know what to do. What would you have done? Tell me what to do to make it right? Please."

Karl couldn't look at her. She'd just condemned her entire species to extinction.

"Goodbye, Lindsey."

Karl ended the transmission. Then he made one final call.

The holographic image of his father appeared in Karl's room. His dad's ruined figure was strewn on a ramshackle hospital bed, like a starship's broken hull on a debris field.

"Dad?" Karl asked, a tear running down his cheek.

"Son? Is…that…you?" his father said in short, labored breaths.

"It is. Dad, I don't have much time. I lost my job, so I won't be able to come home."

"Wha? Can't…you…inter…view…for…another…one?"

"Dad, that's not important anymore. I need you and mom to leave Earth ASAP. I don't care how much it costs. Just leave."

"Why? I…won't…be here…much…longer."

Karl couldn't stand it. "Please, dad. If not you, at least get mom out of there. In a few months, Earth will be gone. Please. Do it for me."

His dad's image winked out, replaced by a spinning credit accompanied with an annoyingly pleasant female voice. "Your credits have expired. Please deposit more credits to continue your transmission. Your credits have expired. Please dep…"

Karl threw his shoe at the holographic projector and cursed. He just hoped his father heeded the advice. Then Karl had a terrifying thought: *That was the last time I'll ever speak to my dad, and I didn't even say goodbye or tell him I loved him.*

Then Karl remembered his call with Glorglin Ugoglin at Mandrake and Wormwood. Perhaps his father had been right after all.

৪৩

"Why are you leaving Screwtape Rearden?" Glorglin Ugoglin asked.

Karl was the most prepared for and most worried about this question. He'd decided positively spun honesty was the best approach. "My employer asked me to work on a transaction that conflicted with my values. In the end, I chose my values and accepted the consequences."

"So you were fired?"

"I didn't say that. I was laid off. My firm eliminated my position."

"I see," Ugoglin said in a tone that Karl thought was tinged with skepticism, though he knew he shouldn't anthropomorphize alien emotions.

"Look, I'd be happy to provide you with any number of references including one from my previous employer," Karl bluffed. He had no idea what Rango might say about him.

Ugoglin hesitated, and then said, "Why don't I introduce you to George Hernandez, our senior banker."

"George Hernandez?"

"Yes, do you know him?"

"No. I'm just surprised to hear a human name."

"Well, we are an equal opportunity employer," Ugoglin said.

"I'm sorry, that wasn't what I was implying. I'm actually pleased to interview for a position working under a fellow human."

"Alright then. Please wait here, while I get Mr. Hernandez."

A tall, meticulously-groomed man entered the room. Karl almost laughed. George had the stereotypical plastic smile of twenty-first-century banking lore. With one glance, Karl knew exactly how he could influence Hernandez. Hernandez wouldn't be interested in Karl's charm or competence. Karl would have to offer him something tangible.

George extended Karl his hand. The handshake was tepid. Karl surmised that Hernandez had no more substance than a used car salesman. In other words, he was probably an excellent banker. "Glorglin tells me you're out of a job."

"That's right. Did he tell you why?"

"Not really. Why don't you tell me?"

Karl had to tread carefully. If he told George about the transaction, Karl would signal that he was an untrustworthy employee. If he said too little, he'd never attract George's interest. "The last transaction I worked on posed a bit of an ethical dilemma for me."

"Don't all transactions pose ethical dilemmas? After all, many of the buyers of the worlds we broker lay off millions of people."

"How many of them result in genocide?"

George's eyes widened. "Tell me more."

"I can't. I'm bound by certain confidentiality agreements," Karl said, playing coy.

"I think the horrors of genocide trump those agreements, don't you?"

Were George's words born of greed or conscience? It didn't matter. George had given Karl license to disclose what he knew.

"The Centaurans are buying Earth."

George's polyurethane grin became real, "Not anymore. Welcome to the team, Mr. Reeves."

౮

The Board of the Transworld Joint Stock Conglomerate convened in an office across from Screwtape Rearden's building. The directors wore the most expensive suits highlighting the latest fashions. They represented a host of economic interests spanning twelve stellar systems and seventeen worlds including Earth. Not one director was human.

When Rango entered, his neck frill flared when he saw Karl seated across the table from the board members. Karl smiled in return. *Not today you greedy genocidal maniac. Not today.*

Lindsey followed Rango. She glanced sheepishly at Karl, but otherwise avoided eye contact.

George Hernandez rose to shake Rango's hand. "Welcome, Mr. Rango. My apologies for the long delay. I'm sorry I had to break up your prior arrangement with the Centaurans. However, I'm sure you understand that it's in my client's best interest to solicit other bids."

"I see," Rango said. "On what criteria will you be basing your decision?"

Hernandez turned to Karl. "Mr. Reeves?"

Karl smiled and then addressed Rango in the most condescending tone he could muster. "Well, Mr. Xen, there are several criteria. The number one criterion is price. However, there are other conditions. For instance, Transworld has no desire to sell its asset to anyone contemplating genocide."

"Whoa! Hold on, here. Who said anything about genocide?" Rango's neck frill flared.

George smiled. "Mr. Reeves is just using genocide as an extreme example. As you'll notice in our due diligence packet, we will require any buyer to sign off on certain pledges to protect the seller from certain reputational risks. For instance, it would be difficult for Transworld to ensure maximum output of its remaining worlds if the firm were to sell an asset to say, a genocidal species. Wouldn't you agree?"

ᘔ

Karl's tenure at Mandrake and Wormwood was short-lived. He lacked the stomach for it. Yet he left in the firm's good graces and returned to Earth with all expenses paid by the planet's denizens after his role in preventing the planet's sale became public. Karl's father had passed away long before then, but had survived long enough to see his boy become a hero and to tell his son he loved him. For that, Karl was thankful.

END

Afterword

A 2012 *Asimov's* story by Indrapramit Das entitled "Weep for Day" originally inspired this tale. While the notion of a tidally locked world – where only one hemisphere of a planet ever sees sunlight, and the other is always shrouded in darkness – is not a new one in science fact or fiction, "Weep for Day" is the first short story I read that explored the concept in an engaging and thoughtful manner. "White Nights, Mammon's City" is radically different than Das's story, but it similarly imagines life on a tidally locked world. More specifically, it explores how such a world would be ideal for a future interstellar investment banking industry.

The first job I had out of business school was as an associate at an investment bank. It was a lucrative job with incredibly long hours. As a former military officer, I was confident I could handle the hours – and I did. But what I didn't realize is that the Army's culture is the antithesis of investment banking culture. In the latter, colleagues and co-workers sometimes exploited core Army values like loyalty, teamwork, and honesty to gain an advantage. In many cases being a team player and accepting responsibility for others' mistakes could hurt you. In contrast, the military expected officers to assume responsibility for their subordinates' actions, and teamwork was essential for survival.

The experience was a real eye-opener for me, and the only analogue I could find in literature that adequately described investment banking culture was C.S. Lewis's *The Screwtape Letters*. In that book, Lewis envisions Hell as a bureaucracy, where the ultimate goal of every devil was to devour souls. C.S. Lewis tells the story through a series of letters between Screwtape, a senior tempter, and Wormwood, Screwtape's protégé. The mood and content of the letters felt very similar to the morally reversed world I had experienced in investment banking. When Wormwood fails to win his human "patient's" soul, other devils consume Wormwood's essence to punish him. Instead of feeling upset about his pupil's fate as any responsible mentor should, Screwtape gleefully insinuates that he will participate in Wormwood's devouring. For, in Hell, it is every devil for himself.

I saw similar behavior at an investment bank in the wake of the 2008 Financial Crisis. I had watched as senior bankers shed junior employees who'd slaved for them for ninety-plus hour workweeks without any shred of remorse. Not everyone behaved this way, of course, but enough of them did that it fundamentally altered my view of humanity.

This story's allusions to Mammon, Screwtape, and Wormwood are not-so-subtle linkages between the literary conception of Hell and the real world of investment banking. Karl only survives by framing his needs in terms of others' interests, because that's the only way to get things done in such a hyper-Darwinian and politically charged culture.

The title of this piece is also an oblique reference to *Bright Lights, Big City*, a novel by Jay McInerney in which the protagonist is caught up in the hedonistic, fast-paced, materialistic, and drug-fueled culture of mid-1980s New York City. The need for humans to use stimulants to compete with the native Reticulans who, owing to millions of years of evolution, did not need sleep, is a nod to that novel. The term "white nights" is an obvious play on "bright lights" and refers to Zeta Reticulum B's never-ending daylight on its sunward side.

This story was first published in September 2014 in Issue 28 of *NewMyths.com*. I hope this story provided some insight into the strange and masochistic world of investment banking, and was also an entertaining read.

Alien Abattoir

"Civilization and anarchy are only seven meals apart"
— Spanish proverb

The wheels on Tom Ehrlicher's hand truck squeaked as he carted the severed heads from Conveyor Five to Conveyor Six. Fluorescent lights flickered as the plant hummed at full capacity in a slaughterhouse that was a model of operational efficiency. Fans whirled overhead to keep the facility's stench from festering. Raptorian carcasses hung from sliding meat hooks lining the ceiling in neat, orderly rows as dark green fluid dribbled from headless stumps into troughs below. The technicians hung the light blue-scaled bodies torso first so that Alpha Centauri Prime's one-point-one gee gravity could accelerate the exsanguination process.

Tom was middle-aged, with spiky, short brown hair exhibiting the telltale signs of male pattern baldness. He had a round gut. His arms and legs were thin and frail, especially for an Alpha Centauri Prime human. Tom's long, horse-like face screamed weakness and tended to draw bullies to him like iron filings to a loadstone. He preferred to keep to himself as his interactions with people rarely ended well.

Tall, muscular Lucius Lundgren, the plant manager, held his chin at a tilt in a classic alpha male dominance display. He acted as if he were a silver-backed gorilla from the vids Tom spent his free time watching. Lucius hurled his daily stream of abuse at Tom. "Hurry up, piss bird. We have to process seventy-five Raptorians this shift. If you spent more time exercising instead of jerking off to your Earth vids, you wouldn't be so pathetic and slow. I have a shift to run and heads to process. People will starve if this factory fails to meet its quota. We can't afford to jaw jack all day."

We wouldn't be jaw jacking if you let me do my job instead of giving me crap, Tom thought, but meekly replied, "You're right, Lucius. I will work harder to get the heads processed on time."

"You're damn right you will." Lucius said and then returned to his platform on a catwalk above the factory floor.

Tom admitted to himself that Lucius' hostility was not without some merit. Tom made too many mistakes on the processing line. Mistakes here got people killed. Not directly, of course, but any time a technician made an error, it could jeopardize the colony's scarce food supply.

No one enjoyed eating Raptorian meat. Tom's grandmother used to say its taste reminded her of beef jerky wrapped in sandpaper. But the colony had no choice.

Even though the technicians at Conveyor Five had decapitated the Raptorians several minutes ago, the Raptorian heads' cranial nerves were still firing rapidly. No matter how many times Tom transported the heads through the plant, he could never shake the feeling that they were watching him.

Each time he picked up a new batch of heads, a wave of raw emotion washed over him. It screamed terror. It had been fifteen years since the colony assigned him this job, but only a few months since he'd started sensing these emotions.

Tom had started hearing the whispers about five months ago after a Raptorian bit him. Well, he didn't really *hear* the whispers. It was closer to a feeling accompanied by flashing images in his mind. If he'd been following procedure and had worn gloves at the time, he'd probably be fine today. But when he took the abuse he did from Lucius, the last thing he wanted to do was to tell the man he'd disregarded regulations. So Tom kept his mouth shut.

As Tom carted his heads to Conveyor Six, the whispers bored into his mind, making it nearly impossible for him to push forward. The emotions were agonizing. Tom had a throbbing migraine as they chipped away at the inner cavity of his skull. It didn't help that the plant smelled worse than usual today. From Lucius' rather colorful language over the intercom system, it appeared some of the fans had broken.

Looking down from his management platform, Lucius seemed more irritable than normal. He squinted his eyes, glaring at Tom. "What's wrong with you, cue ball?"

Lucius didn't wait for an answer. He hopped down from his platform and confronted Tom.

"You feel sorry for the meat, don't you?" Lucius jabbed his sausage finger at Tom's shoulder. "Sometimes you softies forget how the Raptorians welcomed us here – attacking our grandparents. Imagine waking up after being in stasis for over forty years, then having to face wild packs of bloodthirsty lizards."

Lucius pushed his face to within inches of Tom's. "Our grandparents were humane. They stunned these wild animals, removed them, and then left 'em alone."

Lucius forced Tom against a wall. "Then our grandparents found arsenic in everything. In the dirt, in the plants, in the water. They knew everyone would starve within weeks if they couldn't find uncontaminated food. It turned out their ship's hydroponics lab had survived the crash only to be destroyed by the greasy scalies. The creatures also demolished the expedition's communications array, making it impossible to alert Earth."

"Get…off…me," Tom wheezed as Lucius continued to apply pressure to Tom's chest.

"Not 'til I'm finished boy. And wouldn't ya know? It just so happens that the one thing, the only wretched species on this God-forsaken rock that our grandparents *could* eat turned out to be responsible for having destroyed the ship's only food source. Talk about poetic justice."

Lucius glared at Tom then added, "Besides. What else would we eat? Without the scalies, we'd all be dead in three weeks. When you lose focus, you put the whole colony at risk. If there is the slightest hint of an arsenic release when we remove a Raptorian's intestinal pouch, the whole day's batch is lost. You need to pull yourself together. Understand?"

Tom nodded. Lucius was an ass, but he was right.

ۦ

The dome lights were flashing and a high-pitched alarm reverberated throughout the plant. Tom had finished unloading his cart at Conveyor Six when Lucius waved him over to the management platform. "Suit up, Ehrlicher. We have contamination on Conveyer Three."

"Shouldn't Anderson be handling it?" Tom asked. The instant the words left his mouth, Tom knew he said the wrong thing.

Lucius jumped down from the platform and got into Tom's face. "I don't give a rat's ass who *you* think should be handling it. All that matters is what *I* think. And I think you need to put on your clean suit and mop up Raptorian shit."

"Yes, sir."

Conveyor Three was about two hundred meters from Conveyor Six, separated by a steel wall preventing the Raptorians from seeing their compatriots get harvested. It was best to keep them calm and quiescent so the men could process them efficiently.

When Tom arrived at Conveyor Three, Jonas Anderson was already busy cleaning up. Anderson was nearly six feet, tall for someone who grew up in Alpha Centauri Prime's high gravity environment. He was well built, had sandy blonde hair, and a jagged scar on his left cheek. He rarely smiled, but carried himself with a calm confidence that inspired loyalty.

"It's about time you got here, Ehrlicher," Anderson said. "We've got a ton of crap to clean up. I've never seen the scalies act this way when they hit the relaxer. They're usually calm. Five minutes ago about ten of 'em just started freaking out and crapping on the floor. Now the arsenic levels are through the roof. We've got to clean it up – ASAP!"

"It must be the fans. Five of 'em had mechanical failures about an hour ago. These Raptorians must've smelled the others we processed earlier this morning," Tom said.

Anderson nodded. "I suppose so. Lucius is already on it. He started chewing Halls' ass the moment the fan indicator lights went off."

As Tom assisted Anderson, a tempest of emotions overwhelmed Tom. Dry heaving, he dropped to his knees. He convulsed violently as images overloaded his mind. *Panic. Struggle. Death.*

Anderson threw his suction tube down in disgust and started railing at Tom in a litany of profanity. Tom was oblivious to it as the images buffeted his mind.

When Lucius found Tom thrashing on the floor, he ordered five technicians to suit up and drag Tom out of the processing plant. They took him to the loading dock to teach him a lesson, beating him savagely.

ଚ

Tom awoke in a cold sweat. He lay in a hospital bed, emotions swirling. Aggression, anger, and violence coalesced into a single emotive cadence that cycled through his mind. The air was tinged with a thinking violence.

Casts bound both his arms and legs. A bandage extended from the back of his head over his left eye, and ended near his shattered nose. His breathing was labored and not under his control. The respirator beside his bed dictated the pace of his rhythmic breathing.

His hazy one-eyed vision slowly resolved into a solitary figure towering above him. As Tom became more lucid, the face staring at him twisted into a sneer.

"Lucius?" Tom said.

"Little Tommy. It's great to see you didn't die on us. That would've been unfortunate, especially with all the paperwork I'd have to fill out. You know, the 'accident' where the Raptorians went rabid and beat you into a bloody pulp," Lucius said.

"But that's not what happened..." Tom protested in weak, labored breaths.

"Shut up." Lucius walked to the respirator that kept Tom alive. "I hear these things have a high failure rate since most of 'em were made forty years ago and cobbled together from starship parts.

"I repeat: the Raptorians went rabid and tore you apart. There were five other witnesses. It also looks like you suffered some brain damage. Memories get fuzzy when you take some lumps on the head, you know?"

Before Tom could respond, visions flooded his mind.

The emotional maelstrom in his head took shape. Emotions became ideas; ideas became words; words strung together became phrases. *Kill the flesh eaters; flee toward the mountains,* the feelings whispered from the ether.

All was becoming clear.

"Raptorian got your tongue?" Lucius said.

Tom was terrified, but had the presence of mind to realize he needed to warn the colony. "Lucius, what happened isn't important, but what's about to happen is."

"Look, nutjob, I don't give a rat's ass what you think as long as you stick to the party line. You got it? A lot of folks are gonna be on three-quarter's rations because of you. We had to destroy the entire batch today. Arsenic contamination. If you'd done your job, we wouldn't be in this mess."

"Lucius, you've got to warn the colony. The Raptorians are gonna try to escape. People might get hurt. I think they are more intelligent than we think they are."

Lucius shook his head in contempt. "You must've hit your head harder than I thought. Next, you'll start claiming the scalies are making spaceships. Phfft." He laughed then left the room.

&

A soundless, but piercing scream woke Tom at sunrise. *Make violence.*

Blaring sirens interrupted morning's peace and joined the cacophony of voiceless emotions in Tom's mind.

The flashing images told the tale. Forty-eight Raptorians en route from the hatchery to the processing plant attacked their ten handlers. The handlers, conditioned to expect docility from the reptiles, lost control of their cargo.

Tom saw the Raptorians exiting the five-ton meat wagon in columns of two as they always have. Without warning, the thrashing began. The Raptorians surprised their captors, slashing at eyes and throats. Three men were on the ground desperately trying to stem torrents of blood erupting from their jugulars. Seven human survivors subdued several reptiles with electrostatic prods.

More images: Raptorians slashing at human survivors; Raptorians sprinting toward the mountains. Those who fled projected confusion. The hatchery was the only place they'd ever known. The world beyond was a frightening enigma.

Sharp images of pain ripped through Tom's mind. The humans were gaining the upper hand. Fifteen Raptorians littered the ground. Men radioed for aid.

The images became increasingly wild and chaotic. Raptorians streamed toward the horizon. Feelings of freedom's euphoria mixed with desperate pangs of abject terror.

The humans reacted quickly. Dust rose behind the Raptorians as six-wheeled mobiles gave them chase. Retractable nets stretched toward the fleeing Raptorians, ensnaring them.

The open ground soon receded into a vast and rugged *wadi* system etched into the desolate desert landscape from centuries of periodic flash flooding.

A loud bang roused Tom from his visions. Looming in the now-open entrance to Tom's hospital room was a dark, brooding silhouette.

"You tipped off the Raptorians, didn't you?" Lucius pointed his finger at Tom to underscore his accusation. "You knew this was going to happen. You wanted it to happen. And now you're going to pay, you smug little runt."

"I tried to warn you..." Tom said.

Lucius leered over Tom and backhanded him across the face, knocking a tooth loose. "Shut up! If you tell anyone that story, they'll call you crazy and you know it. I'll deny it too. But how the hell did you know they were going to do it?"

"I dunno. I can't explain it. I just felt it in my mind."

"You really are crazy. But, little Tommy, it don't matter neither way. We've lost twenty-five Raptorians to the wild today. Our food supplies are dangerously close to going below the colony's minimum subsistence level. If there were another accident, we'd have to start cutting colony rations to fifty percent. The way I see it, we need to capture more Raptorians. Since you're probably responsible for this mess, I volunteered you to join the war party as soon as you're discharged from the hospital. I hope you know how to fight. The wild Raptorians you're gonna be hunting ain't the submissive hatchery variety. They're the kind that bites back."

"But we shouldn't be eating them. They're sentient beings," Tom said.

"That's crap," Lucius said. "They're nothing but food."

৪১

Lucius selected ten men for the hunting party and organized them into five-man teams. Each team would travel in one of the colony's six-wheeled, all-terrain mobiles. Each hunter carried two service rifles – one, a three-hundred-shot mini-rail gun for personal protection, and the other, a long-range electrostatic stun rifle for subduing feral Raptorians. None had any prior hunting experience. Their only source of knowledge was their grandparents' half-century-old tales about a near fatal encounter with the Raptorians.

Lucius seemed upset he couldn't join the expedition. His reaction wasn't all that surprising to Tom since the man seemed to have an unsettling love of violence. Nevertheless, duty called. He had to oversee the meat processing plant's shutdown and subsequent investigation. Tom was just relieved he wouldn't have Lucius there to second-guess Tom's every move.

Jonas Anderson would lead the expedition since he was closest thing to a warrior the colony had. After the original settlers drove the Raptorians across the mountains, decades of uninterrupted peace had ensued. A need to maximize food output and a lack of imminent threats had rendered the military profession obsolete. The colony shepherded the majority of its resources for food production.

Anderson's grandfather was the only colonist who'd had any military experience. Before becoming an astronaut on Earth, Jonas' grandfather had flown hovercopters for the United States Army during China's Great Collapse in 2097. He also had single-handedly organized a hasty defense of the colonists' perimeter when the Raptorians first attacked. Nearly shattered by the experience, he taught his son, Anderson's father, everything he knew about military doctrine and tactics. Anderson's father, in turn, had passed some of those lessons on to Jonas.

Today, Anderson's usual self-confidence seemed shaky to Tom. It appeared as if Anderson regretted not having paid more attention to his father's stories. Tom hoped Anderson could get over his fears of inadequacy because the men needed strong leadership. If Anderson lost hope, the other nine would as well. Jonas had that way about him, possessing a confidence-inspiring aura that could bolster courage in the most craven of cowards.

The men began their mission at dawn, or at least as close to dawn as Alpha Centauri Prime came in its binary star system. Night here was more like permanent twilight since Alpha Centauri B, the second sun, appeared nearly two hundred to twenty-five hundred times brighter than a full moon on Earth.

The mobiles lumbered toward Anderson Pass, nestled in between the mountains towering in the distance. The first colonists named it in honor of Anderson's grandfather who had chased the Raptorian packs through it then sealed it off decades ago to protect the colony.

As the Alpha Centauri A sun set, Anderson ordered the men to decamp for the evening. They set up a laager site near a large rock outcropping.

Anderson signaled the men to gather around him at the side of his mobile. "Each of us is going to pull a two-hour shift in teams of two. If you hear or see anything, alert me immediately. Then wake everyone else. Every man should sleep with his rifle within easy reach. There's no telling what can sneak up on us out here. Also, do nothing alone. If you need to cop a squat, take another man with you. Always operate in two-man teams. In fact, let's formalize them now."

Anderson called out names and paired each man with a battle buddy. "Foster!"

"Yeah!"

"You're with Ehrlicher."

Foster whined, "How'd I get stuck with the village idiot?"

Laughter followed. Tom just shrugged. *This is going to be a long trip.*

ം

"Wake up, tubby!" Foster shook Tom in his sleeping bag. "It's time for our shift. If you fall asleep on me, so help me God, I will end you."

Tom was freezing. In this continent's arid climate, temperatures could drop by as much as sixty degrees Fahrenheit from day to night. Tom's frozen breath and perspiration had caked his sleeping bag in frost during the night. His uncontrollable shivering made donning his socks and boots a struggle.

Foster seemed impatient with Tom's lethargy. "Hurry up, you slug. We have a perimeter to watch."

Tom climbed to the top of his mobile and surveyed his assigned sector, while Foster occupied the roof of the other mobile on the opposite side of the perimeter.

The night passed slowly – agonizingly so. Besides the hurried rush of Alpha Centauri desert beetles scurrying on the ground, the evening was quiet. Tom's mind was calm. He was certain nothing dangerous lurked in the twilight. He didn't know why he felt that way. He just knew.

"You hear that?" Foster whispered over the radio, his voice on the edge of panic.

"Yeah. It sounded like some rustling in the bushes. It's probably just the wind again," Tom said.

"Are you dense, man? Can't you hear that? It's getting louder. Listen."

Tom listened with his ears and opened his mind. His thoughts were still, yet the rustling grew louder. Moments later, he heard a metallic click. Foster had jammed a rail gun cartridge into place.

Something trudged up the gravelly slope near the perimeter's edge. It would soon emerge from the murk.

Foster's tension was contagious. "Foster, I'm heading over to your position," Tom whispered. Tom slid down from his mobile and crept towards Foster's mobile.

Foster nodded. Then he lowered his eyes to his rail gun's sight, aiming at the thing in the gloom. It all became clear when Tom reached the other mobile.

"Wait! Noooo!"

A blue flash of light heralded the rail gun's sharp recoil as tiny metallic pellets traveling at a fraction of the speed of light disintegrated Charlie Jones, leaving no trace of his existence save wisps of vapor and heat, and a pile of ash.

Foster turned to Tom and said, "It's his own stupid fault. He had to go out and take a dump without his battle buddy. Anderson told everyone not to do anything without taking a battle buddy."

&

Nine men erected a makeshift headstone where Jones fell. Anderson seemed pissed. It was a stupid way to lose someone. The incident underscored his advice about staying in pairs.

Foster became a leper for his impulsive actions. For the first time in Tom's life, Tom no longer felt like the runt of the litter. That distinction now belonged to Foster. Anderson reassigned Tom to a new partner, a taciturn fellow named Jim Collins.

&

Be the female, lure the male, the whispers lulled in melodic suggestion. To Tom, it felt like the calm before a storm. He stirred in his sleeping bag against the newly awakened voices in his head. Twilight's cold made him shiver, but memory heightened his renewed awareness.

Two days before, the expedition had passed through the man-made barriers at Anderson Pass without incident. The team had discovered that the fuel cells powering the electromagnetic fields keeping the Raptorians from crossing the pass had malfunctioned since the last scheduled maintenance check eleven months prior. Nothing had protected the colony since. They'd been lucky. When Anderson returned home, he'd have to plan a second expedition back to the pass so the engineers could fix the problem. The team he had today had neither the time nor the proper equipment to perform the task.

Dense forest and brush on the mountains' windward side forced the men to leave their mobiles on the far side of the pass. The men made their way on foot toward Alpha Centauri Prime's Great Sea. Precipitation here was far greater than that on the mountain's leeward side. After two days of forced marching, the men's feet were blistered, raw, and bloody.

The murmurs in Tom's mind increased in frequency and intensity. Tom now had enough experience with these portents to know he had to steel himself and alert the others. In minutes he was on his feet and armed. He moved briskly through the camp, waking his comrades.

For the first time in Tom's life, he felt he could influence others. He'd also learned that after Lucius had returned from Tom's hospital bed, Lucius had ridiculed Tom in front of the technicians for Tom's strange premonition about the Raptorians. The men all had laughed. When the Raptorians escaped, the men seemed no longer to find Tom's visions so funny. After a long hike through this strange and menacing wilderness, the men were now downright superstitious, most believing Tom had some sort of sixth sense.

The camp became a hive of activity as men donned their body armor and loaded their magazines. The nine checked and rechecked their weapons. As they moved to secure their camp's perimeter, the first hail of arrows sailed into the campsite's center. Horns blared in the distance and a mass of Raptorians streamed toward the campsite from the south.

Many of the men reacted by freezing in place, needlessly exposing themselves to the flurry of arrows. It was though a herd of wild cattle somehow organized, clothed themselves, and attacked them with spears. It simply never entered the realm of possibility that animals would fashion tools and assail humans with them.

Anderson's presence of mind was the only thing that prevented the Raptorians from slaughtering everyone. He directed six hunters to hit the ground and fire their weapons into the ambush. He ordered the remaining two colonists, including Tom, to position themselves perpendicular to the edge of the ambush line, forming an "L". He wanted to blunt any potential Raptorian surprise attacks from the hunters' flank.

Wave after wave of Raptorians crashed upon the defenders with crude spears, but the rail guns made short work of them. Still, the Raptorians advanced despite the grievous damage the men wrought against the reptiles' ranks.

"Tom, tell me everything you're sensing. How many Raptorians are out there? What's their objective?" Anderson asked.

Tom concentrated hard. *Gnash with teeth. Sting with tail.* The same vision played over and over in his mind.

"It's tough to translate, but I think they've fixed our force on our right and are preparing to outflank us at our current position," Tom said.

"Are you sure?"

"It's tough to tell. I don't hear words. I just see images and feel emotions. Now, I see a lizard snapping at its prey, while it coils its tail, preparing for a fatal blow."

Anderson shook his head decisively. "Well, that's clear enough for me. Estrada, Haley, and Betts, pull back. Assemble at my location."

The men obeyed Anderson's orders and prepared their fighting positions.

"Here they come!" Haley yelled.

A fresh wave of Raptorians assaulted from a new direction, in front of Tom's position. While the Raptorians continued their attack on the men to Tom's right, it was becoming clear that they were investing their main effort in this flanking maneuver.

Tom fired a rail gun for the first time in his life at a Raptorian rushing not twenty feet in front of him. The velocity of the electromagnetically propelled pellet disintegrated his target. The immediacy of the attack gave Tom no time to process the memory. He just pointed, aimed, and shot at anything that moved within thirty feet of his position.

After about twenty minutes of fighting, but what seemed more like twenty hours, the Raptorians broke off their attack.

Anderson pushed the upper half of his body up with his arms to get a better view of the Raptorians. After surveying the scene for about a minute, he stood up, and assessed the expedition's tactical situation. "Is everyone okay?"

Everyone nodded. The most serious injury was a broken arm. Halls had hit the ground too hard after the arrows had started flying into the perimeter.

"How're we doing on ammo?" Anderson asked.

Everyone had several three hundred round rail gun cartridges left.

"Halls, stay behind and watch our gear." Anderson said.

"Sure, boss," Halls said.

"OK, gents, let's counterattack these bastards!" Anderson ordered.

The men looked at Anderson as if he were insane. None of them had been in combat before and he was asking them to do more. Moreover, the realization that they weren't facing mindless animals, but rather a self-aware species capable of fashioning weapons and devising rudimentary military tactics was unnerving.

Anderson looked at Tom. "What are you seeing?"

Tom's mind was flooded with chaotic images of men vaporizing Raptorians and Raptorians scrambling away. He felt their terror. "They're retreating."

Anderson turned his attention to the others. "If there's any time we can catch the scalies with their pants down, it's now. Whaddya say, boys?"

They all agreed and the hunt was on.

The men swept through the forest in a horizontal line, blasting any Raptorians they encountered on their path. The thoughts and images the Raptorians projected into the ether seemed increasingly desperate and terrifying to Tom. With each burst in image intensity, a rifle shot invariably followed as the expedition killed another Raptorian.

After nearly half an hour of pursuit, Anderson raised his right fist and took a knee. The other seven men halted and took cover. He motioned for them to gather around him.

"Solid work, gents," Anderson declared. "But we still haven't accomplished our mission. We're here to capture some of these critters alive so our people don't starve. Now that we have the advantage, let's chase the surviving Raptorians back to their nest. There, we should be able to surprise them and gather the livestock we need.

"Estrada, radio Halls and let him know what we'll be doing. Tell him we'll return within twenty-four hours. If we don't return, he's to head back to base and return with reinforcements, even if it's every able-bodied adult left in the colony."

"Will do, boss," Estrada said.

"Boss, quick question?" Haley asked.

"Go ahead."

Haley appeared distraught. "These Raptorians had armor, bows and arrows, and spears. I thought they were supposed to be mindless animals. What the hell's going on?"

"Yeah, I had the same question," Anderson said. "The Raptorians have apparently come a long way in fifty years from naked animals to weapon-wielding savages. These bastards are probably a heck of a lot smarter than we've given 'em credit for. That means you gents should be on your toes the next time we face 'em. Never underestimate your enemy."

"Wait, Anderson," Tom interrupted. "Maybe we should head back. The Raptorians are sentient beings. That changes everything."

Anderson stood in quiet contemplation, eyes fixed on the ground. After a long silence, he rendered his decision: "It changes nothing. If we don't eat them, we die. It's that simple."

ॐ

The hill the hunters chose for their observation post provided an excellent view of the burrows leading to the vast network of subterranean Raptorian nests. The nests were embedded in a string of tree-lined hills. For someone with no military experience, Anderson seemed to have internalized his father's lessons well. The group planned to execute a snatch-and-grab mission once Alpha Centauri Prime's primary sun was directly behind the men's backs. If the Raptorians sallied out to oppose them, they'd be fighting into the sun's blinding rays.

Sadness. Regret. Loss. A visual compilation of background noise kept a constant vigil in Tom's mind. Unprompted, Tom looked over his shoulder at Anderson and said, "They're grieving."

"Excellent," Anderson responded. "Haley, do you have the electrostatic nets ready?"

"I do."

"Alright." Anderson nodded. "Let's go."

The men raced down the slope toward the nearest burrow. Two men remained at its entrance to provide rear security for the six-man snatch-and-grab team. Tom joined Anderson at the column's vanguard to provide him with advanced warning of the Raptorians.

Wrong. Infection. Unclean, the visions showed Tom.

"They know we're here," Tom whispered to Anderson.

"I'm not surprised," Anderson said. "What does surprise me is that they haven't tried to attack us yet."

"They've probably got nobody left," Haley said.

Remove. Exterminate. Kill, the images screamed.

"Get ready, they're coming!" Tom yelled.

The men dropped to the ground and found whatever cover they could. Movement echoed throughout the burrow's ribbed walls.

Armor-clad Raptorians stormed at them, launching bronze-tipped javelins. The men returned fired with their stun weapons, neutralizing the Raptorians moments before the lizards overran them. Raptorian bodies quickly piled up and clogged the tunnel.

"Betts, Haley, haul the stunned Raptorians outside. Queue up the maglev field devices so they're ready for transporting the cargo. Net them in groups of thirty. Once we hit about one-twenty, we're out of here," Anderson ordered.

Betts and Haley carried out the order, while the remaining four men kept watch for signs of another Raptorian attack. It was about three tense hours before the area was completely clear of unconscious Raptorians. In the interim, the Raptorians who had been struggling to get at the men from tunnel beyond appeared to have left the scene.

"How many you got?" Anderson asked.

"Twenty-two," Haley answered.

"OK. That's not gonna be enough," Anderson said. "Let's see if we can get closer to the queen's hatchery to steal some of her eggs. They should be lighter than full-grown Raptorians and won't fight back."

The men wended their way deeper into the bowels of the Raptorian nest. The farther they ventured, the more the moisture level increased.

Fear. Panic. Terror, flooded Tom's mind. "We're almost there. The Raptorian warriors that remain will rally around the queen."

The men rounded a corner where the narrow tunnel emptied into a vast chamber housing a massive and bloated Raptorian queen. She roosted upon hundreds of bluish green eggs. Dozens of heavily armored warriors surrounded her in a protective barrier.

Another violent exchange ensued, but the humans with their superior weaponry made quick work of the Raptorians. In a last ditch effort to ensure her progeny survived, the queen lunged at the men, only to be rendered inert with several stun blasts.

Anderson ordered the men to gather as many eggs as they could carry. They packed the eggs into the electrostatic nets and attached the nets to several maglev field devices that made the eggs' transport back to base possible for a small team.

∞

"Well, well, well. Mr. Hero," Lucius sneered. "If you think I'm going to treat you any differently, you got another thing coming, little man."

"Go away, Lucius," Tom said.

Lucius puffed up his chest and rushed over to Tom, thrusting his meaty finger into Tom's face. "What did you say, you pathetic little maggot?"

Tom glared at Lucius, Tom's eyes boring directly into Lucius'. He repeated his words, taking care to enunciate each one. "Go. Away. Lucius."

Tom's legs gave way. A loud crack echoed throughout the plant. Blood sprayed from Tom's nose, which was now contorted in an impossible angle. Within seconds, Lucius was on top of Tom pounding away at him with his fists, as Tom lay helpless on the plant floor.

"Anderson! Halls! Haley! Betts! Collins! Estrada! Help me!" Tom pleaded.

All these men, Tom's battle companions, sprinted to the scene and…watched. Tom could see the tension on Anderson's face fighting between loyalty to his comrade-in-arms and fear of his boss. He had to choose between the manager of the plant that fed his family and the man that saved his life. He only needed one of them now. Every man had the same conflicted look on his face. Nevertheless, Anderson was the group's leader. Whatever his decision, the group would follow.

After what seemed an eternity to Tom, Anderson finally interceded. "Lucius, enough! You're going to kill him."

Anderson's warning seemed to rouse Lucius from his stupor of fury. Lucius got off Tom's broken body and shoved Anderson before stomping out of the plant.

"Help…me. Please, help…me," Tom gurgled as he writhed on the floor. Spittle mixed with blood trailing from his mouth. His torn face was a rictus of agony. "Don't let me die here. Please."

His comrades said nothing. They did nothing. Not one could bring himself to look Tom in the eyes. Instead, they just walked away.

Tom lay mired in his own blood and filth for hours, harboring a dark melancholy. He realized it no longer mattered what he did. Life would never improve for him.

A tidal wave of psychic energy suddenly buffeted Tom's mind. His eyes rolled back into his head and he convulsed in an epileptic fit. The images he saw filled him with foreboding. Thousands of Raptorians poured over the mountains through the malfunctioning barrier. The images reminded him of the vids he had seen of an old Earth locust plague. Nest upon nest, they were coming to reclaim their missing. Tom knew their numbers were so vast they exceeded the colony's ammunition caches. The Raptorian horde would overwhelm the colony within a week.

It was at that moment that Tom figured how to turn his life around. He knew what he had to do.

ℯ

Procuring a stun gun from the colony's arms room was easier than Tom had expected. "Anderson, please, let me borrow it. It will protect me from Lucius, and prevent any more violence on the plant floor. Surely, you and the boys don't want to clean up another bloody mess? Plus, I've already been in recovery for a few days. The plant can't afford me off work again just because Lucius can't keep his cool," Tom reasoned.

Anderson appeared skeptical, but Tom pressed his case. "You saw Lucius in there. If something sets him off like that again, he'd probably kill me. If I carried a weapon, he'd be more likely to back off. Besides, you owe me for our time in the field. I saved your life – help me protect mine."

"You know I can't give you a weapon. I'll tell you what. If I were to discover my arms room key, which I keep in my plant office, is missing, I would be deeply upset. However, I don't plan on checking the second desk drawer on the left any time in the next few hours. You catch my drift?"

"I have no idea what you're talking about." Tom smiled.

෨

The next morning, the images and emotions swirling in Tom's mind grew more frequent and urgent. The Raptorians were close. Very close. They'd already traversed through Anderson Pass, and would be at the colony by day's end.

Tom waited tensely for the meat wagon of colony-raised Raptorians to arrive. When it did, Bob Rogers halted the vehicle in front of the plant's loading dock. There, the handlers would herd the Raptorians onto ramps leading into the plant. After the handlers entered the back of wagon to gather the captives, Rogers turned his head and noticed Tom. Rogers hit the dirt before the man had a chance to notice Tom's stun rifle.

The nine others hadn't seen Bob drop. They were too busy in the meat wagon's passenger compartment to notice. Tom crept to the side of the vehicle where he expected the handlers to exit.

Tom blasted Steve Chen before his feet reached the ground. Tom jumped several feet, turned, and ran into the vehicle's open hatch, taking out three more men on his way up.

When Tom arrived, there was a panic inside the crew compartment. The remaining six handlers scrambled to get away from Tom and toward the emergency exit on the floor. Tom stunned the men one by one until he had subdued them all.

Tom then projected his memories of his work on the assembly line toward the back of the meat wagon.

Fear. Panic. Terror, blanketed him in eddying waves. He responded with images of the open plain then sent the Raptorians a visual description of his plan for their freedom. It had the calming effect Tom had hoped for.

Tom dashed to the arms room adjacent to the processing plant. Using Anderson's key, Tom removed ten more stun guns from the weapons rack. When Tom tried to use Anderson's key to unlock the rail guns, it didn't work. Then he noticed several were missing. Tom never had intended to use the rail guns himself, but had planned to hide them so that the other men couldn't use them against him. That Anderson denied Tom access to these weapons showed Tom that Anderson was craftier and more cautious than Tom had expected.

Tom returned to the meat wagon, throwing open the back hatch. The Raptorians waiting there eyed him suspiciously, though they made no move to attack him.

Tom pointed his stun rifle away from the vehicle and toward the empty plain, firing one silent energy burst. He then handed a second stun rifle to the closest Raptorian. He motioned the creature to emulate his actions. The Raptorian did. They understood.

Lucius and the boys never knew what hit them. Expecting a group of forty-eight docile Raptorians, the men inside the abattoir got a rude awakening.

The Raptorians made short work of the humans as they advanced through the plant. They incapacitated all the technicians, save Anderson and Lucius.

While Lucius was a demeaning bully, he possessed a unique talent for survival. It was no surprise to Tom that he shadowed Anderson like a hawk.

When two Raptorians disintegrated before him, the degree to which Tom had underestimated Anderson became clear.

Tom visualized Anderson's face and his smell in his mind's eye. The telepathic signal was so effective that even the unarmed Raptorians suddenly sprung into action. It was one human and forty-six Raptorians to two men, only one of whom posed a serious threat.

Anderson and Lucius were holed up on Lucius' platform. The Raptorians advanced toward them from all directions. It was only a matter of time before the Raptorians ripped them to shreds.

Anderson blasted away at the advancing Raptorians with his rail gun. In seconds, he reduced ten more into ash before they could sink their claws into him. In the end, the law of large numbers won out. Anderson couldn't hold out against such long odds.

The surviving Raptorians restrained Anderson and Lucius, forcing them up against the wall. Tom approached the two men and signaled the Raptorians not to harm them.

"I always knew you were a Raptorian lover, you backstabbing bastard," Lucius said.

Tom rammed the butt of his stun rifle into Lucius' face, breaking Lucius' nose in a hard snap, and taking three teeth with it. "Shut your trap. I'm in charge now."

Anderson took a more rational approach. "Tom, please, think this through."

"I did," Tom said. "I really did."

"Seriously," Anderson pleaded. "When all this is over, what're you going to eat?"

Tom ignored Anderson's question. Before the feral Raptorians arrived, he had to cement his status as a human they could trust. He sent the others images about how to operate Conveyors One through Six.

The Raptorians restraining Lucius lifted him up and carried him toward Conveyor One.

"No, no, nooooo!" Lucius squealed like a pig ripe for slaughter. "Tom, please. I'm sorry. I swear it! Please, don't do this. Please!"

∞

Lucius' head cleared Conveyor Six when thousands of the feral Raptorians arrived. The liberated Raptorians signaled trust to calm the martial impulses of the outsiders, enraged by the destruction of one of their nests.

Humanity's fate on this world dangled by a thread as Tom sought to reverse three generations of unwitting sacrilege against a sentient race.

All must be punished, the Raptorian hive mind projected. *Only you have earned mercy.*

Tom projected, *Humans can provide you with medicine and technology. If you help us with our request, we will gladly help you thrive on this world.*

What is your request? the hive mind thought.

Before I answer, I ask one question of you, Tom answered with a thought. *How do you honor your dead?*

Puzzlement and confusion met Tom's request. He tried again. *What happens when members of your clan stop eating, drinking, moving, and thinking?*

We let them lie where they fall, the hive replied, *unless they fall in the nest. Then we take them out to the forest and let nature consume them.*

Tom sent another thought. *Our request is that you send the older members of your nests to us when they are near death. We promise to treat them well here until they die. We will then become nature and consume them.*

Anderson seemed to have understood the crude and utilitarian calculus of Tom's plan. Given the numbers and the circumstances, Tom doubted

Anderson could've come up with a better solution. The colony's future hinged on this singular moment.

After some consideration, the hive mind projected one final thought.

෨

The relief mission had left nearly five years after the final transmission of the colony ship destined for Alpha Centauri Prime. Traveling at one-tenth the speed of light, it had taken the mission forty-four years for the relief vessel to arrive.

When the starship landed near the colony, the settlement appeared empty and lifeless. Yet, a single solitary figure approached the vessel from the plains. He was a feral-looking man, half-starved and near death, but clinging tenaciously to life nonetheless.

END

Afterword

"Alien Abattoir" was the fourth speculative fiction story I wrote, and the third story I began submitting to various markets. An earlier version of this story earned an Honorable Mention in the Writers of the Future Contest's third quarter of 2012. That said, when I workshopped the story with former *Clarkesworld* editor, Nick Mamatas, he pointed out that it had a number of problems. For one, it could be at least a third shorter without the long middle section where the group raids a Raptorian hive. Second, the story has too much exposition. Additionally, Nick suggested that the story seems to have some tonal problems with what he viewed as an almost comical interaction between Tom and Lucius in the beginning. Then the story gets dark until the Raptorian hunt in the long middle of the story, where things lighten up. Then the story ends on a much darker note.

My wife had a far more negative reaction than Nick did. The initial images of the story disgusted her to the point that she had refused to read any further. That's one of the major challenges in writing speculative fiction: every reader is unique and each person sees a story through different lenses.

While I fixed many of the original story's logical inconsistencies, I left this story largely unaltered from the version that won an Honorable Mention in the Writers of the Future Contest. After all, despite its obvious limitations, something about it worked for contest judge, David Wolverton.

Either way, the concept for this story is one of my favorites. I hope you enjoyed reading it.

Remember New Roanoke

Two roiling suns scorched the desert landscape as the gaunt man stumbled toward the bivouac site. Commodore Tina Morales wiped the sweat off her brow and took another glimpse through her binos. More bone than man, the colonist seemed almost feral. His shredded and grimy olive drab coveralls hung from his skeletal frame like a parachute.

The commodore had planned to send an expedition out to New Roanoke within forty-eight hours. She'd wanted to go sooner, but her command team had needed time to analyze the probes' data.

Keying the comms device secured around her right ear, she said, "Reaper Six, this is Falcon Six, SITREP. Over."

"Falcon Six. Reaper Six. Wait One," Colonel Carlson replied.

She rolled her eyes. Space marines. Any chance they had to assert their authority over a fleet officer, they took it. Still, she was the highest-ranking officer on the expedition. Her only crime was she wasn't a space marine, but she played along, because she needed them more than they needed her. "Reaper Six. Standing By."

"Falcon Six. Identified male survivor at five-point-zero klicks and closing. Permission to engage with lethal force?"

Carlson had always been trigger happy, but this request was absurd. She was convinced he was the wrong man for this mission. She needed a ground commander who saw the world in shades of gray, not through a black and white prism.

She keyed her comms device. "Negative. Stand down. Acknowledge."

"Negative. Contact could be infected. Over."

An alien pathogen was a logical hypothesis. Over the last fifty years, something had reduced the colony's population from the two hundred and fifty souls on the original colony ship's manifest to fewer than ten.

What Morales found even more intriguing were the thousands of heat signatures remote probes had detected beyond the eastern mountains, but remote DNA spectral analysis had determined there was no human genetic material there, so Admiral Chu had limited operations to within fifty klicks of New Roanoke.

The intel was a one-time deal. The *United Earth Ship Eldridge* would be moving on toward the nearest star in twenty-four hours. After that, the expedition would be on its own and Morales would be in charge.

"Reaper Six. Engage with stun weapons only. Acknowledge."

A long pause followed. "Acknowledged."

"Reaper Six. Give me a SITREP in fifteen minutes. Out."

Two six-wheeled mobiles carrying a space marine platoon streamed past. The marines seemed frisky this morning, almost too frisky. They'd never operated in a one-point-one gee environment before, and she worried their bodies might break before their enthusiasm did.

Morales surveyed the horizon. She still couldn't get over seeing two suns in Alpha Centauri Prime's sky, and knowing that somewhere out there laid the answer to the great mystery that had spurred her parents to leave Earth in an interstellar generation ship forty-four years earlier. Three quarters of the crew had been born in space, and this was the first time most of them, including her, had ever set foot on a terrestrial surface.

၈၃

The starveling huddled in a field tent about a hundred meters from the marines' mobile compound. Morales entered the tent with the marine battalion's intelligence officer, Captain Aram Berberian. Both wore their sleek light-refracting environmental suits and protective masks. Three folding chairs surrounded a square table dominating the tent's center.

The horse-faced man rocked in his metal chair at an irregular cadence, his balding skull cradled in his arms. Morales looked at Berberian. "Has he been treated for heatstroke?"

Berberian nodded. "Yes, ma'am. He's fine. A lack of water isn't his problem."

"Well, he didn't survive out here without eating something. I wonder what's changed," she said.

Pulling out a nutrition bar, she offered it to the man. He stared at the offering with bloodshot eyes sunk deep in black sockets. The tent was so quiet she could hear her heart beating. Then the man lurched forward, snatched the bar and devoured it.

"What happened to your settlement?" Berberian asked. "Why did it stop sending signals to earth?"

She held up her hand: too many questions. They needed to ease him into the interrogation.

Berberian tried again. "We're just here to help. Why weren't you with the other colonists?"

The man remained silent, twitching and rolling his eyes.

"Look, we've come to investigate what happened here," she said, "We haven't heard from your people in over forty years. If I can't get answers from you, I'm gonna send marines into your settlement to find out myself. My marines are among the finest, but they make mistakes too. I'd hate for someone to get hurt because of a simple misunderstanding."

The survivor looked down. His twitching intensified. "P-P-Please don't. Your men could get infected."

Inclining her head toward Berberian, she said, "I'll be damned. Carlson was right."

"As you can see," she said to the colonist, gesturing at her environmental suit, "we're prepared for that. Unless you cooperate, we're going to the colony."

The colonist's twitching escalated to quaking. His eyes rolled into the back of his head. Then he bit her, ripping a hole into her suit and savaging her arm before she could knock him to the ground.

Her heart raced, but she took a deep breath. "Captain Berberian, as of fifteen hundred hours local time, you and I are on quarantine. Order a detachment to seal off this field tent. Radio Major Jones, report the incident, and request full medical examinations for both of us."

Berberian did as instructed, and Major Jones arrived within the hour.

"Commodore Morales, my apologies for the delay. We had to erect secondary and tertiary containment structures around the field tent."

She nodded.

"What happened to him?" Jones pointed at the unconscious man.

"I gave him a little love pat after he took a chunk out of my arm." She smirked.

Jones nodded. "Commodore Morales, please remove your environmental suit."

"You sure that's a good idea?"

"If this man's carrying anything, you already have it. Your suit's just gonna get in the way."

"Fair enough." She removed her suit, and then turned her head toward Berberian. "What about him?"

"Did the subject bite him too?"

"No."

"Then it's unlikely he's been exposed. His suit stays on."

Jones pulled out a foot-long cylinder the thickness of a human thumb. "Stand at attention," he said to her.

"Aren't I supposed to say that to you?" she said. The humorless doctor showed no reaction. He pressed a button on his device and a light source emanated from it, scanning her from head to toe. The doctor projected an image of her vital functions in the air accompanied by a detailed readout of her medical condition.

"Am I okay, doc?"

"Stand by," the major said as he processed the medical information. "Respiratory and cardiovascular systems are operating within normal parameters. Lymphatic and endocrine systems are also functioning normally. No signs of any harmful astro-bacteria. No foreign toxins in your system. It looks like you have a clean bill of…wait a minute. What's this?"

Morales tried to hide her anxiety. "I'm going to need a little bit more than that, major."

Jones pointed at the hologram. His thumb and forefinger grasped the three-dimensional cross section of her skull like a pincer, and then released it to expand the image. Jones pressed an icon below the hologram and a detailed rendering of her brain appeared. Jones pointed at two almond-shaped structures above the brain stem. "See these microscopic growths here on your amygdalae?"

"My what?"

"Your amygdalae. These two kidney-shaped structures process emotions and help store long-term memories."

"Bottom line this for me, doc."

"Well, ma'am, the good news is that the virus in your system is dormant. The bad news is that it's triggered the growth of these nodules, and I don't know when they'll stop growing. While their growth rate has decelerated,

I'm going to insist you confine yourself to quarters until I can ensure your safety."

"Is it contagious?"

"Yes. You can transmit it from exposure to your blood or via sexual intercourse," Jones said.

"If I don't go around biting people, mixing blood with them, or sleeping with them, can it spread?"

"Well, technically, no, but I insist that…"

"Negative, doc. That'll be all. Dismissed."

Jones turned to Berberian, but Berberian just shrugged.

"Major, I gave you an order. Dismissed!"

Jones snapped to attention, rendered his salute, and left.

℘

By the time Alpha Centauri Prime's primary sun pierced the horizon, the marines' mission to New Roanoke was well underway. Morales had decided to tag along despite Colonel Carslon's protests.

Major Jones was required to keep her medical diagnosis confidential, but Captain Berberian wasn't, and rumors of her medical prognosis had spread through the marines like a virus.

Morales shared a mobile with a marine squad, and the marines kept their distance. They were a superstitious bunch, but she decided not to force the issue. That they didn't panic when she entered their mobile was an encouraging sign.

The mission objective was to secure a facility on the colony's outskirts. Towering above the colony's other buildings, the structure's solitary and soot-encrusted smokestack stretched toward the sky. Remote probes had indicated that the settlement's remaining heat signatures were concentrated there. Twenty-four mobiles carrying nearly three hundred marines, or nearly two-thirds of all combat power on Alpha Centauri Prime, headed toward the objective. It seemed like overkill to Morales, but she deferred operational planning to Carlson as he was the expert on such matters.

A small marine contingent had cleared out an adjacent outbuilding before she arrived. She listened to the radio traffic as they reported their discovery: an empty arms room with storage racks designed for stun weapons and rail guns.

Her mobile positioned itself fifty meters from the facility's hanger doors several minutes later. Through her mobile's periscope, Morales watched as the rear exit ramps of two nearby mobiles dropped to the ground and two marines lumbered through the gravity soup toward the hanger.

They attached explosive gel on a locked hanger door, embedded a quantum sensor in the gel and trudged away from the target. Seconds later, a rectangular, man-sized breach burned through the door.

"Falcon Six. Reaper Six. I'm taking a team into the building. SITREP to follow. Over."

"Reaper Six. Falcon Six. Roger. Out."

She watched the five men disappear into the facility, and waited.

"Falcon Six. There's something you need to see."

"Reaper Six. Report."

"Negative. You need to see this in person."

Morales found Carlson's request out of character. He normally didn't bother to filter his thoughts. She descended the ramp of her dark mobile, the blinding light and blistering heat of the planet's primary sun overloading her senses.

She plodded toward the breach, and entered, stumbling as her eyes adjusted again to the darkness. The area stank of rot and putrescence.

"Commodore Morales, over here!" Carlson shouted.

She followed his voice, while her eyes struggled to adapt. A vision of the factory slowly coalesced. Metallic meat hooks dangling above stainless steel troughs lined the ceiling in orderly rows. A conveyor system wended its way through the plant, culminating in a human-sized, cube-shaped machine. A single steel platform rose above the plant floor.

At the far end of the facility, the marines were assembled in a horseshoe. Carlson turned his head. His eyes locked with hers, then he looked away and pointed beyond the semicircle of fazed marines.

Children.

Huddled, shaking, and emaciated, the kids were nothing but bone bags covered in tatters. There were five: three boys and two girls. Their ages seemed to range from about three to twelve. All had haunted looks in their eyes, the veneer of innocence long since corrupted, twisted, and exposed for a lie. They reeked of filth.

Morales labored to remain calm despite overwhelming feelings of nausea. "Colonel Carlson, get these children to a medic."

Carlson nodded and relayed the order over the net. Five more marines arrived and escorted the children outside. Carlson gestured toward those who remained. "Clear out the rest of this shit hole. Send a SITREP every ten minutes."

The marines saluted and moved out. Carlson turned back to her. "Your orders?"

She wasn't expecting that. She was hoping she'd have some personal time to get herself together.

"Let's see what your marines learn," she said, "then we'll decide what to do next. Once we get those children some medical attention and food, we'll ask them what happened here."

"Those children need some serious psychological help. They need an interrogation like I need the clap."

"Well that shouldn't be a problem since you've already got it, Carlson."

Carlson chuckled, but then his voice took on a more serious tone. "Commodore, what is this place?"

"Some kinda slaughterhouse." She pointed at the meat hooks. "The colonists probably hung the animals up there and let the blood collect into the troughs below. I'll betcha dollars to donuts that whatever they ate had something to do with those thermal signatures beyond the mountains."

Carlson nodded, but his eyes seemed elsewhere. "Why would anyone bring children here? What kinda sick fuck does that?"

"The kind we already have in custody."

Carlson grinned.

"Don't get any ideas," she said, then pointed at the block-shaped machine, "Any idea what that's for?"

"No clue. All I know is that the spectral analysis my marines ran on it showed an unusually high concentration of arsenic. Seven hundred times higher than the arsenic concentration in the surrounding soil, which is fifty times higher than Earth's."

The battalion net squawked with a transmission. "Reaper Six. This is Warlock Three. You gotta see this, sir."

Carlson glanced at her and then extended his arm in a direction leading deeper into the facility. "Ladies first."

The two walked past rows of meat hooks until they reached a massive steel partition. Making their way through the partition door, they passed several tables holding a variety of worn cutting and carving implements.

"Warlock Three. Reaper Six. Talk to me."

"Reaper Six. We're inside a refrigeration unit. Break. Once you pass through the first partition, there're double doors at the far right end of the building. Break. You'll find us there."

"Acknowledged, Warlock Three. We're on the way. Out."

Morales saw the double doors ahead. She advanced slowly, her curiosity pushing her forward, but a sense of foreboding holding her back.

She pushed open the doors to find the four marines at the rear of the refrigeration unit. Scores of frosted blue-scaled torsos dangled from meat hooks.

She found the sight unsettling, but no more disturbing than the beef held on meat lockers on the *Eldridge*. Yet, the marines at the far end of the corridor stood sullenly, facing away from their discovery.

"C'mon, it's just lizard meat," Carlson said, appearing to have rediscovered his swagger.

"It ain't about the lizard meat, sir," a marine said, then he pointed up. "This is why we called."

She looked up and saw more torsos. Human torsos.

℃

"Who murdered those people, you twisted bastard?" Berberian said, leaning toward the man the children called "Uncle Tom".

No response.

"Why'd you lie about the pathogen?" Morales asked.

The colony's sole adult survivor stared into space. She was losing hope. The man refused to talk no matter what they did, and the children hadn't been much better. They'd only offered their names and identified Tom. Otherwise, they were all but comatose.

She pounded her fists on the table. "Dammit! Why are there human remains in the meat locker?"

Tom smiled. His eyes locked on hers. *Fear. Anger. Vengeance.* A train of images followed. *The abattoir. Reptilian heads on hand carts. Men in coveralls beating on Tom. Squat, light-blue reptilians firing rail guns at men.* The torrent of images assailing her mind faded as suddenly as they began, but she felt a lingering sense of revulsion.

Tom broke his silence with maniacal laughter. "You fools!" He giggled. "They're coming! He-he! They're coming! Ha-ha!"

"Who's coming?" Berberian said.

"You'll see! And you'll be sorry you ever messed with 'ole Tom Ehrlicher."

Faster than she could react, Tom jumped up on the table and began dancing. "Ha-ha! He-he! They're coming for me! Just wait and see! Just wait and see! Ha-ha! He-he!"

Berberian grabbed his stun pistol and applied two hundred and fifty kilovolts to Tom's sternum. Tom fell backward, hitting the hard sand, his body convulsing.

&

"Wake up, ma'am, Colonel Carlson needs to see you ASAP."

Morales opened her eyes to see a burly, ginger-haired marine standing beside her cot. "Whaah?" she said, half asleep, "Why?"

"I'm not at liberty to discuss it, ma'am."

She didn't like the sound of that. "Excuse me? I outrank the colonel. Anything he knows, I know. Why does he need to see me?"

The marine pointed his shock lance at her. "I'm sorry, ma'am, but you're coming with me."

"Goddammit, marine! I give the orders around here, and I'm ordering you to put down your weapon." She stormed toward him until his weapon touched her chest. "I'm not going anywhere."

The marine lowered his weapon and then keyed his comms device. "Reaper Six, this is Thunder Three. Over."

She was close enough to hear the reply on the marine's earpiece. "Thunder Three, Reaper Six. Send it."

"Falcon Six refuses your orders. Permission to engage. Over."

"Permission to engage?" Morales yelled. "You kidding me?"

"Thunder Three. Negative. Heading to your location, time now. Out."

She glared at the marine. "Boy, I'm gonna have your ass when this is all over."

She turned and grabbed her khakis. The marine just watched. She dressed quickly, though she took care to tie her hair into a neat little bun. Maintaining her military bearing was more important now than ever.

Moments later, Colonel Carlson arrived with two stocky marines in toe. "Commodore Morales, by order of the Uniform Code of Military Justice, I declare you unfit for duty. I am…"

"Bullshit!" She cut in. "This is mutiny, Carlson. Calling it anything else is like putting lipstick on a pig."

Carlson continued. "I'm assuming command of this detachment until Major Jones can provide you with a clean bill of health. You'll be confined to quarters until further notice. That is all."

Clenching her fist, she ran toward Carlson. She felt a blow to the head. Then everything faded to black.

ʚɞ

Morales awoke in a cold sweat. Intense afterimages of clinical decapitation seared into her mind without reason or context. She struggled for meaning.

A cursory glance at her surroundings confirmed her worst fears. The marines hadn't confined her to her quarters. They'd thrown her into the brig.

A wave of someone else's emotions flooded into her mind. And Tom was at the center of it all. She watched Tom wheel a cart of severed reptilian heads through the abattoir as dark green fluid dribbled from man-sized lizard carcasses on meat hooks. She saw a severed head bite Tom in a final nerve-spasmed gasp, and with it felt a new awareness. She experienced the escalating bullying of Tom as he struggled to describe his visions and the unsettling truth of Raptorian sentience to others who refused to understand or accept it. Storms of anguish and suffering battered her psyche, pushing her to sanity's brink.

She descended further into Ehrlicher's madness. She watched him become the conduit between the hives and humanity. When the hives beyond the mountains had learned the colonists were eating their kind, they sent their swarms toward the gleaming city upon the hill. Convinced that the Raptorians would ultimately overwhelm the colonists with superior numbers, Tom freed the Raptorians bred in captivity and subjugated his own people in the hope that it would appease the hives.

Morales watched in horror as Tom collaborated with the Raptorians to corral the colonists. Predator became prey. As a reward for his service the Raptorian hive minds had allowed Ehrlicher to eat their dead, but the logistics of traversing the eastern mountains had proved difficult for one human adult and his prepubescent workforce. So Tom had had to choose which colonists would live and who would be eaten. Each processed human was a ticking clock. As the colonists' numbers dwindled so too did Tom's projected lifespan.

She knew Ehrlicher was a monster, but she still pitied him. Then more visions came, filtered through Tom's mind, but alien and born of a collective consciousness. Thousands of Raptorians streamed over a mountain pass armed with spears and rudimentary armor toward the cursed desert city.

Morales screamed.

Within seconds a marine sentry entered her cell. "What's going on?"

"Get Colonel Carlson. Immediately."

The marine shook his head. "I'm sorry, but that ain't gonna happen. He's busy."

"Dammit, marine, that's an order, not a request."

"I don't take orders from you anymore."

Falling to the floor, she screeched louder. The marine hesitated, and then tried to lift her off the ground.

Morales kneed him in the groin. He toppled over, wheezing. She slammed his head against the floor, knocking him unconscious. Grabbing the marine's shock lance, she sprinted from her cell, stunning a second marine rushing toward her.

She removed the comms device from the downed marine and broadcast over the battalion net. "Reaper Six. This is Falcon Six. Report." The instant the words left her mouth, she knew she'd made a mistake. Carlson wouldn't respond to an order.

Then she reconsidered. *No. Screw him*, she thought. *I'm in charge.*

"Reaper Six. This is Falcon Six. You have thirty minutes to report to the brig to answer for charges of mutiny and sedition. Break. As you know, a defendant found guilty of mutiny, sedition, or failure to suppress or report a mutiny or sedition shall be punished by death or such other punishment as a court-martial may direct. Break. If you cooperate, I will waive the death penalty. Over."

"Prisoner Two. This is Reaper Six. Surrender immediately, or I will use deadly force to put you down. Out."

"Reaper Six. You now have twenty-nine minutes. Out."

Morales knew she had no way of reestablishing her authority now, but she needed to warn Carlson about what was coming.

The marines stormed the brig. She stunned five before they took her down.

She woke tied to a chair with a beaming Carlson seated across from her. "Well, well. You bested seven of my marines. Pretty good for a space squid."

"Cut the crap, Carlson. And it's Commodore Morales to you."

Carlson rolled his eyes. "Don't piss on my cornflakes and call it milk. Did you really think you could bust outta my brig or that my marines would follow you over me?"

"No. I just wanted your attention."

"You sure as hell succeeded. Did you call me to plead for your release, to tell me you're no longer infected?"

"No. I need to warn you. There are tens of thousands of the creatures we found in the abattoir coming here to wipe us out."

Carlson laughed so hard he nearly fell out of his chair. "Now I know you're a one hundred percent certifiable, class one whackjob. You constructed an elaborate fairy tale using a whiff of real intel."

"So I'm right. Your sensors are picking up movement over the mountains."

Carlson smirked, then his jaw tightened. "That's no longer your concern."

"Carlson. Hear me out. Send me out there. I can broker a deal and convince them we have enough food to prove we're not a threat."

Carlson chuckled. "You're telling me they think we're here to eat them? How the hell do you know that?"

She couldn't tell him the truth. It was too preposterous. "Ehrlicher can communicate with them."

"Bullshit. You said *you* could broker a deal, not Ehrlicher."

"It doesn't matter. Send me out there. Best case I come back with an agreement that avoids a fight. Worst case they kill me. Either way, you win."

Carlson grinned. "Who said I wanted to avoid a fight?"

She lost it. "Are you insane? You think three hundred marines can stop tens of thousands of sentient creatures evolved to fight in one-point-one gees?"

"Oorah!"

Morales couldn't decide whether Carlson was stupid or mad, but his response left little room for interpretation.

She had only one option.

Her thoughts reached out beyond the compound, and sought out a mind so mad, she doubted she could find any remnant of sanity. Receiving thoughts had become painless for her, but transmitting them required more effort than she'd imagined. Yet, she pushed on, sending images of the bivouac site with the locations of all marine sentries, the way to the compound, and the path to the brig. Blood dripped from her nostrils as her head throbbed from the strain.

A response emerged from the ether. *I'm coming.*

୫୬

Days later, shortly after twilight, Morales's cell door opened. Tom entered with the five children.

"Why did you bring them?" she said, glancing at the children, "Our work will require stealth."

Tom grimaced. His thoughts entered her mind. *We're the only ones who will survive. If I leave them here, they will die with the rest.*

She answered, *The Raptorians will understand reason. We can show them we have our own food here, and we mean them no harm.*

No. The thought's emotional finality betrayed Tom's madness. *Do you think I wanted to eat the others? I had no choice.*

She didn't respond. It was pointless arguing with a madman. She just needed his help to get to the Raptorians.

How'd you get here so quickly? Morales projected.

The marines are using every available fighter to defend the colony's perimeter. They left you locked here without a guard. I faked another epileptic episode and my guard bought it.

How'd you know what the marines were doing? You were under guard.

The hives told me. They have binos too.

Then she remembered the empty arms room. *My God,* she thought, *they have rail guns.*

Tom smiled.

She led Tom to the compound's arms room, where she punched in her code into a wall-mounted keypad. A light scanned her retina, and then a door opened.

I can't believe that bastard didn't change the access codes, she thought. She grabbed two shock lances, handing one to Tom.

When they emerged from the compound, the area was deserted, but Morales saw a riot of activity in the distance as marines dug trenches, unrolled concertina wire, and installed automated spider mines. She was certain the marines would wrack up an impressive body count, but she was convinced the Raptorians would ultimately overwhelm them. Yet, she was still hopeful she could prevent a confrontation.

She led Tom and the children into the desert. After four hours of slogging through sand, she reoriented the group in a direction that would skirt New Roanoke's eastern outskirts, providing them with a five-kilometer buffer to avoid tripping any remote defense systems.

The group meandered through sand dunes until the primary sun rose in the east, where its orange hemisphere illuminated a limitless stream of Raptorians funneling onto the valley floor.

Morales looked west, where she saw two armored mobiles heading in her direction, churning clouds of dust in their wake.

Waves of bloodlust washed over her. She broadcast her thoughts to the hive, pleading for mercy, but she might as well have tried reasoning with an earthquake.

The air rippled with the sonic boomlets of rail gun rounds streaming overhead toward the Raptorians. A little girl screamed. The other children held their hands over their ears, while Tom cackled with insanity.

Morales dove for the dirt, motioning for the others to follow. The children complied, but Tom ignored her, babbling incoherently.

The mobiles would be at their location in minutes.

The ground rumbled from the footfalls of thousands. Morales strained to reach the Raptorians. *Please. Peace. Talk.* She sent images of their starship, their lives, and their food stores.

The mobiles stopped within two hundred meters of her position. Carlson emerged from an exit ramp, armed with a rail gun. He crawled across the open plain, firing his weapon. His first shot landed near Tom, tearing a three-foot crater into the earth. Tom lost his footing and fell, and then another sonic boom heralded his disintegration.

Morales made one final plea to the hive minds, and in an instant, thousands ground to a halt. Then, a single Raptorian made its way toward her.

The air crackled as the Raptorian fired a round at Carlson. She watched as Carlson exchanged fire with the Raptorian. Using the distraction, she aimed her shock lance at Carlson, fired and missed.

Two squads of marines joined Carlson in the firefight. She took another shot, and missed. Another marine returned fire. Carlson fired again at the Raptorian. She glanced behind her and saw a whiff of smoke where the Raptorian had been standing. Then the ground began to shake as the Raptorians resumed their march.

Towers of sand exploded before Morales as more marines targeted her. She returned fire, stunning two marines. The children screamed. A little blonde girl panicked and bolted toward the Raptorians and a marine turned her to ash.

A tear rolled down Morales's cheek as she struggled to suppress what she'd just witnessed. *What have we become?* she thought.

The marines appeared to have similar reactions and ceased fire. Carlson waved a white flag. She waved back. Carlson motioned for her to come forward, so she crawled across no-man's land hoping for a peaceful solution. When she arrived, Carlson smiled and recited her previous words, "A defendant found guilty of mutiny, sedition, or failure to suppress or report a mutiny or sedition shall be punished by death."

Then he pulled the trigger.

END

Afterword

I wrote "Remember New Roanoke" in reaction to a critique from Nick Mamatas on the previous story, "Alien Abattoir" as part of his excellent speculative fiction writing course in Berkeley, California. I enrolled in Nick's course because he had a reputation for brutal honesty, especially during his time as an editor at *Clarkesworld*. While some thin-skinned authors have reacted to his criticisms as off-putting, I found them refreshing because he always backed them up with copious evidence and suggestions for improvement.

Nick's suggestions for "Alien Abattoir" were numerous and helpful. In the end, he recommended that I rewrite it entirely. "Remember New Roanoke" was my answer to that critique. That said, I didn't want to scrap "Alien Abattoir" entirely since an earlier version of the story had won an Honorable Mention in the Writers of the Future Contest. However, I did want to explore the concept from a different point of view. What if the colony's rescuers had discovered Tom Ehrlicher after he'd turned on the colonists? How would the rescue party respond to the horrors of his mechanized cannibalism? How would the Raptorians react to a second wave of human colonists? The result was what I think is a more chilling "Remember New Roanoke".

I am convinced that because this "Remember New Roanoke" incorporated many of Nick's techniques from the workshop, the story sold quickly to *The Colored Lens* in 2013. In fact, the story sold so quickly that two of the most prominent science fiction magazines, *Asimov's* and *Analog*, never saw it because I had been waiting for them to review other stories.

Either way, "Remember New Roanoke" is one of my favorites, and I hope you liked it.

About the Author

Sean Hazlett is a technology analyst and fiction writer who has published over two hundred research reports on clean energy, semiconductors, and enterprise software including Wall Street's first comprehensive market analysis of opportunities in the smart grid, which was cited twice in *The Economist* (See "Making Every Drop Count" and "Smart Grids: Wiser Wires"). His fiction has appeared in *Plasma Frequency Magazine, The Colored Lens, NewMyths.com, Fictionvale Magazine, Outposts of Beyond,* and *Mad Scientist Journal.*

Before becoming a technology analyst, Sean was a research associate at the Harvard-Stanford Preventive Defense Project where he worked on energy security issues that included the United States-India Strategic Partnership and policy options for confronting Iran's nuclear program. He won the 2006 Policy Analysis Exercise Award at the Harvard Kennedy School of Government for his work on policy solutions to Iran's nuclear weapons program. Sean also spent time at Booz Allen Hamilton as an intelligence analyst focusing on strategic war games and simulations for the Pentagon. Before graduate school, Sean was a cavalry officer in the United States Army where he trained American forces for combat operations in Iraq and Afghanistan at the National Training Center.

Sean holds a Master of Business Administration from Harvard Business School, a Master in Public Policy from the Harvard Kennedy School of Government, and bachelor's degrees in History and Electrical Engineering from Stanford University.

www.ingramcontent.com/pod-product-compliance
Lightning Source LLC
Chambersburg PA
CBHW070023120726
47909CB00003B/1045